Time had stopped.

Jenna's gaze was locked with Paolo's, and her awareness was so totally focussed on the man beside her.

As his was. On her.

He lifted his hand, using his middle finger to smooth a blob of soapsuds from just below her eye. The touch was so light, so intense, it could be nothing less than a caress.

The connection unleashed something almost frightening. Jenna wouldn't have believed that Paolo's eyes could darken that much. Or that she would ever hear him utter a sound that was pure, raw desire.

'You,' he said, very softly, 'are beautiful. *Bella*.'

And then Paolo tipped his head and kissed her.

Softly. Slowly.

It wasn't enough. Not nearly enough. And Jenna knew Paolo was thinking exactly the same because her gaze was still locked onto his—as it had been from the first moment he had touched her face.

There was no question of whether or not they would make love. It was simply a matter of when…

Dear Reader

Mills & Boon are celebrating their 100th birthday this year. How amazing is that?

For a whole century readers of romance have been loyal to a genre of fiction that celebrates what I believe matters the most: the relationships between people. Love…

I fall in love with every one of my heroes, but a gorgeous Italian like Paolo in THE SURGEON CLAIMS HIS BRIDE was deliciously irresistible. That means there's a part of me in every heroine, of course, but it's more than just the part that falls in love. I suspect that you also relate to the same ideal. One that recognises the meaning of true love and what is precious about the connections to other people that mean we are not alone in the world. Not simply the magic relationship between lovers—we also cherish the bonds of family and friends. As Paolo and Jenna learn, it is possible to feel utterly vulnerable and yet to feel completely safe at the same time. Maybe that's the essence of feeling loved?

I'm proud to be writing these stories as Mills & Boon enters its second century. May the tradition continue to bring us all moments of joy.

Happy reading

With love

Alison

THE
ITALIAN SURGEON
CLAIMS HIS BRIDE

BY
ALISON ROBERTS

First published in Great Britain 2008
Large Print edition 2008
Harlequin Mills & Boon Limited,
Eton House, 18-24 Paradise Road,
Richmond, Surrey TW9 1SR

CITY
LIBRARY
CORK

6178411

ISBN: 978 0 263 19975 8

Set in Times Roman 16½ on 18½ pt.
17-0908-49866

Printed and bound in Great Britain
by Antony Rowe Ltd, Chippenham, Wiltshire

Alison Roberts lives in Christchurch, New Zealand. She began her working career as a primary school teacher, but now juggles available working hours between writing and active duty as an ambulance officer. Throwing in a large dose of parenting, housework, gardening and pet-minding keeps life busy, and teenage daughter Becky is responsible for an increasing number of days spent on equestrian pursuits. Finding time for everything can be a challenge, but the rewards make the effort more than worthwhile.

Recent titles by the same author:

CHRISTMAS BRIDE-TO-BE
THE PLAYBOY DOCTOR'S PROPOSAL†
THE ITALIAN DOCTOR'S PERFECT FAMILY
  (*Mediterranean Doctors*)
A FATHER BEYOND COMPARE*
ONE NIGHT TO WED*
EMERGENCY BABY*

Specialist Emergency Rescue Team
†*Crocodile Creek*

CHAPTER ONE

WHAT the hell was going on here?

It was like a good-cop, bad-cop scenario. Hardly what Jenna Freeman had expected when fronting up to this fabulous old house in Hamilton Drive, one of the most exclusive parts of town, to attend a job interview.

A woman who looked to be in her seventies was beaming at Jenna approvingly. The other woman, twenty years her junior, had fixed Jenna with a steely glare. Both had formidably strong personalities.

'I'm not sure I understand,' Jenna said carefully. 'Is there something wrong with the little girl?'

'With Danielle? Good heavens, no! She's perfect.'

The gazes of all three women shifted automatically to focus on the subject of their conversation and Jenna found herself smiling.

Yes. Danielle did look perfect.

As babies went, this one was a stunner.

Jenna had met a lot of babies in her career as a paediatric nurse and could almost always find something appealing about them. Some looked like they should be advertising baby food in glossy magazines. Others had heart-melting smiles. Some were placid and cuddly and easy to care for, others noisy and fascinated by the world around them.

They were all diffcrent and yet this one— nine-month-old Danielle Romano—was in a class of her own.

She looked ready for a photographer's attention in the beautiful pink smocked dress, long white socks and pristine patent leather shoes. A band that matched her dress squashed some of the silky-looking black curls on her head and sported a bow on top as perfect as the similar decoration on the shiny white shoes.

Small fingers were playing with the bow on one shoe right now. Carefully. As though Danielle was confident she had all the time in the world to explore the shape and feel of the object. The wealth of bright toys surrounding her in the playpen couldn't compete for her interest.

She must have sensed the direction of the women's attention, however, because her fingers stilled and she looked up. Big, dark eyes regarded Jenna with no hint of alarm at the presence of a stranger. There was no hint of a smile either, but that was hardly unexpected, especially in a child serious enough to find the bow on her shoe so compelling.

Jenna's smile faded as she looked back at the women sitting opposite her.

Danielle's grandmothers.

'Your advertisement specified a qualified nurse. Someone experienced with children.'

'That's right.'

'But the position you're describing is looking after a perfectly healthy child. It's a job for a nanny, not a nurse.'

The older of the two women, Maria Romano, looked away quickly, giving an impression of discomfort. If it hadn't been a weird thought, Jenna would have described her as being nervous.

The younger woman, Louise Gibbs, looked almost smug as she nodded less than subtle agreement.

'I said that, Maria,' Louise murmured. 'She's not suitable for the position.'

Not suitable? Jenna bristled. Surely the decision should be hers, given that she was over-qualified for the work being offered. If she took it, she wouldn't be using more than a fraction of the knowledge and skill she had worked hard to attain so far in her career.

'Jenna's more qualified than anyone with just a diploma from a nanny school, Louise. We want the best for Ella, don't we?'

'Danielle.' The correction seemed to be auto-matic. Louise dropped her gaze to Jenna's CV, now lying on the coffee-table between them. 'You're a little younger than I had in mind.'

'I'm thirty-one.' Getting rapidly older, in Jenna's opinion. All her friends seemed to be married and starting families by now. Only Jenna remained single and childless. Destined to silence the ticking of her own biological clock by caring for the children of other people?

Awful thought. Maybe she'd made a mistake even fronting up for this interview. The idea of being a private nurse in a new city had been appealing, however. An easy job. Time to come to terms with the difficult changes life had presented recently and reset herself. A chance to meet new people in a place that wasn't haunted by too many memories.

An old friend she had kept in touch with since they had trained together had applauded the notion.

'*Do* come to Christchurch,' Anne had urged Jenna. 'It would be so good to spend some time together again.'

'And you're single.' Louise made it sound like some kind of disease.

'Yes.' Jenna straightened her back. The last man in her life had done his best to leave her feeling she hadn't made the grade. She wasn't about to let someone's grandmother dent the fragile self-esteem she had managed to restore. 'I wouldn't be applying for a live-in position if I wasn't single.'

'Of course you wouldn't,' Maria agreed. 'And you're quite old enough to be very experienced. How long have you been a paediatric nurse?'

'Six years. And before that I worked in the emergency department.'

'There you go, Louise. Wouldn't it be wonderful to have someone who could cope with any emergency or illness that Ell—Danielle might have?'

Maria's smile was warm. An Italian woman, her English seemed almost flawless, though quite heavily accented, and she used her hands a lot when speaking. She was a little on the plump side and her clothes, while of the best quality, appeared to have been chosen for comfort rather than style. With her lovely smile and hair a natural silver, she reminded Jenna quite strongly of her own mother and so she smiled back with a genuine response to that warmth.

'Hmm.' Louise's gaze was still blatantly assessing and cold enough to provide a startling contrast to the eye contact Jenna had just broken with Maria.

Not that she had to try and hold this gaze. Louise dropped hers deliberately to take in the plain black skirt and blouse Jenna had deemed suitable for this interview and the way her long hair was neatly tied back in a ponytail. It even seemed to take particular note of her lack of jewellery and her short, neatly trimmed, unpainted fingernails.

And then it suggested comprehension of her single status. Annoyingly, Jenna felt a stain of colour touching her cheeks. OK, maybe she wasn't model material like this woman's beautiful grandchild or the gorgeous blonde woman that featured in numerous photographs dotting the mantelpiece of this room, but she wasn't *un*attractive.

Involuntarily, her gaze flicked to one of the larger images. A wedding photograph, which looked too perfect to be real. The man was gorgeous. Tall, dark and in command, with his hand possessively covering the one linked through his arm that belonged to the blonde princess in the cloud of silk and tulle.

There was a resemblance there to the younger of the two women opposite Jenna. More than simply the wealthy, over-groomed look. There was a sharpness to the features that didn't exactly scream warmth. Jenna wasn't at all sure she liked Louise Gibbs and she was rapidly coming to the conclusion that this job wasn't what she was looking for.

She shifted in the chair. 'I feel I may be wasting your time.'

'No, no!' Maria reached out a hand, a gesture designed to pre-empt any further movement on Jenna's part. 'Please, stay.'

For an instant, Jenna saw something new in Maria's face. This was more like fear than nervousness. It was gone too quickly to identify reliably but it resurrected that undeniable curiosity. There was something rather strange about this interview and it would be unsatisfying to leave without discovering what it was.

Jenna stayed put.

'Danielle's father is Paul Romano,' Louise said into the silence. She was watching Jenna carefully. 'A paediatric surgeon here in Christchurch. You will have heard of him, I expect?'

The Paul Romano? Jenna couldn't help looking impressed. He was well known as a specialist in dealing with the removal of childhood tumours. In conjunction with the paediatric oncologists, the reputation was enough to have children sent long distances to receive treatment here.

'Of course. We often referred our more complicated cases here. He's well respected.'

'Yes.' The simple word spoken simultaneously by both women carried a weight of pride.

'Paolo's my son,' Maria added. 'My only child. My only family in this country. Sadly, his father passed away three years ago. We—'

'Paul was married to *my* only child,' Louise interrupted. 'My daughter Gwendolyn. Tragically, she experienced massive complications from an embolism following the Caesarean needed for Danielle's birth and…and she died when Danielle was only three hours old.'

Louise looked away, struggling for control, and Maria tutted sympathetically, murmuring something soothing in Italian as she reached out again, this time to pat her companion's arm. Jenna couldn't help warming to them both.

'I'm very sorry,' she said quietly. 'It must have been a dreadful time for you.'

Louise rallied. 'Paul was devastated, of course.

He still hasn't come to terms with losing Gwen, and having Danielle doesn't help.'

'Oh?' This was puzzling. Surely having a child, a living part of someone you had loved, would be the greatest comfort possible? A man with the intelligence necessary to become such a renowned surgeon couldn't blame the infant for her mother's death or had his love for his wife been such that any reminder could only keep the grief alive?

'Paolo moved home so that I could help with raising Ella,' Maria said.

So this house belonged to the Romano family. Maybe Louise was not a key player after all.

'And I moved to Christchurch.' Louise made it sound as though she was sacrificing more on behalf of her grandaughter. 'Although I would have been—still am—more than happy to take on the full responsibility of raising Danielle.'

The full responsibility? Did the father not have anything to do with his daughter? Were these two grandparents fighting over custody? No wonder there was an odd feel to this household. Doubts about the advisability of working here resurfaced and must have shown on her face.

'It's not that he doesn't love Ella,' Maria said hurriedly. 'It's just that it's been difficult for him. He's always being terribly conscientious about his work and it became an escape for him to put more and more into his career in terms of hours. He's not at home very much.'

'It would be a demanding job.' Jenna looked back at Danielle, who was now busy removing her shoes. 'It's lucky that you are both able to help.'

'As if I'd do anything else.' Louise sounded faintly outraged. 'Danielle is all I have left of my precious daughter. My only child.'

'Paolo was an only child, too,' Maria reminded her. She waved her hand apologetically at Jenna. 'Louise and I are both widows,' she added, as though that explained everything.

Which it did to some extent. This baby was very important to them both as the sole member of the next generation of their families. Jenna was aware of how close Italian families were so Louise must be very determined to keep her stake in Danielle's upbringing.

They were both determined and, for some reason, in competition with each other.

Interpersonal politics could detract from any job. Condensed into an intimate domestic situation that encompassed inevitable cultural differences and included an outsider such as herself could make a working environment intolerable. The warning bells were ringing loud and clear for Jenna.

So did the cry from Danielle. Maria stood up immediately and went to the playpen. The baby held up her arms and Jenna could see it wasn't easy for the older woman to pick her up.

'Oh, dear, you're very wet, aren't you?' Maria cuddled the baby. 'You need a clean nappy, *cara*.'

'I'll do it.' With smooth grace, Louise rose and took the baby, allowing no time for protest. 'You may as well show Jennifer the flat.'

May as well? Was she going to be allowed to view living quarters she wasn't going to be using just to fill in time while Danielle was having her nappy changed?

'Yes, of course!' Maria seemed eager to comply. 'Come with me, Jenna.'

Reluctantly, Jenna followed Maria. The self-contained flat was attached to the vast old house through a short passageway that was accessed through a large, gleaming kitchen. Yet another older woman was busy near the sink. She glanced up curiously as Maria led Jenna across the tiled floor.

'This is Jenna,' Maria said. 'I'm going to show her the flat. I hope she might be joining us to help look after Ella. Jenna, this is Shirley. She helps me in the house. You wouldn't be expected to take on cleaning duties, which I know are expected of some nannies. Or cooking. I love to cook. I teach Italian cookery at the evening classes.'

Shirley gave Jenna an up-and-down glance and clearly liked what she saw. 'You'll like the flat,' she said matter-of-factly. 'Would you like a cup of coffee when you're done?'

'Maybe later,' Maria said. 'When Paolo gets home.' She seemed keen to usher Jenna through the door of what must have originally been servants' quarters.

It had clearly been upgraded considerably. The sitting room was tiny but tastefully decorated and it contained a television, music system and well-stocked bookshelf. The bedroom looked comfortable and there was a sparkling bathroom and a small kitchen area with a microwave and facilities for making tea and coffee.

'You would have complete access to the kitchen, of course. And the laundry,' Maria said. 'There's a—what do you call them? The baby-radio thing?'

'A baby monitor?'

'Yes, thank you. Ella can sometimes be hard to get to sleep but when she is sleeping, she doesn't wake often at night.' Maria raised her eyebrows. 'What do you think?'

Shirley hadn't been mistaken. 'It's a lovely flat,' Jenna said sincerely.

'Do you think you might like to take the position?'

'Ah…' Jenna let her doubts show. 'Can I ask how you've been managing up till now?'

'We had a nanny. She left two days ago. Louise didn't…ah…find her suitable. There was an argument and…' The shrug was eloquent. It suggested that falling out with Louise was a terminal condition.

'Mrs Gibbs obviously doesn't think I'm particularly suitable either.'

'It is not just her decision. It is Paolo who has the final say.' But Maria sighed. She cast a glance over her shoulder at the door she had closed behind them. 'Louise is very protective of Ella,' she said. 'And of Gwendolyn's memory. I'm embarrassed to admit it, but she thinks that any woman who comes into the household is going to…um…'

'Make a play for Danielle's father?' Jenna supplied helpfully. Hardly a suggestion from left field, given the attractions obvious in that wedding photo. Judging by this house, he had a very wealthy background. His fame as a surgeon was another hefty drawcard and his Mediterranean background would be the icing on the cake for some women.

Maria was nodding unhappily. 'Ridiculous, I know. Of course, I hope that Paolo does find someone eventually and that Ella will have brothers and sisters but I suspect Louise is determined that no one is going to try and step into her Gwendolyn's shoes.'

Jenna almost smiled. Talk about offputting. Louise Gibbs would be the mother-in-law from hell, irrespective of whether she was related to her granddaughter's stepmother. 'I can assure you I have absolutely no interest in forming a relationship with any man at this point in my life. I'm very happily single for the moment.'

Which was absolutely true. Jenna wasn't about to complicate her life with the potential for more unhappiness and even if she *was* open to meeting someone, there were a lot of qualities far more important than looks or the state of bank accounts. Intelligence for one. And compassion. And a sense of humour. Tolerance and warmth and…

'So you might consider taking this position?'

Jenna focussed again with a blink. 'I still don't understand quite why you want someone with my qualifications.'

Maria was silent for a moment. And then she gave another small, resigned sigh. 'You've probably noticed that Louise is a lot younger than I am. I was nearly forty when I had Paolo and Gwen was ten years younger than him. Louise is only forty-two. I'm seventy-four and things are not as good as they used to be,' Maria continued quietly. '*Artrite*. Arth-aritis. Another bone thing I can't pronounce.'

'Osteoporosis?'

'Yes.' Maria nodded approvingly. 'I think so. And I have the blood… Oh, what is it? *La pressione alta.*'

Translation seemed surprisingly easy. 'High blood pressure? Hypertension?'

Maria nodded again. '*Si.*' As she relaxed into her confidences, her accent became stronger— her English less perfect. 'And now I have been told I have the diabetes. The bad one.'

'Type one? You need insulin injections?'

'Yes. *Iniezione.* The needles. I have to start them soon. Tomorrow, maybe. I have an appointment with the doctor. It's difficult. Sometimes my English is not as good as it should be for being here in *Nuova Zelanda* for more than twenty years. Shirley has been helping me but she knows no more than I do. We are like—how do you say it? The blind leading the blind.'

At last, Jenna understood at least part of what had made this interview so puzzling. It wasn't the baby who was the potential patient. It was Maria. The older woman touched her arm. It was almost a plea.

'Paolo needs time to get used to being a father by himself. I don't wish him to know that it is difficult for me to help. If we were still in Italy, it would be no problem, of course, but Paolo will not consider leaving his job and families are not the same here, are they? If Ella was taken to Auckland by Louise, she would be lost to us and that would be…a *tragedia*.'

Dark brown eyes that had not faded with age were swimming with tears. 'It's not for me,' Maria said. 'And it's not just that Louise doesn't share the same things of importance in raising a *bambino*. It's because Ella needs her papa. And he needs her. He just hasn't realised it yet.'

In other words, Jenna would be stepping into an emotional minefield. The passions of an Italian family on the one side and a cold and determined woman, possibly obsessed with the memory of her daughter, on the other. Hardly the easy job she had anticipated but it wasn't going to be pleasant to disappoint someone who clearly cared so much about the best interests of others. Especially when one of those 'others' was a baby girl who had no idea of the undercurrents in the world around her.

That concern for others made the reminder of her own mother stronger than ever. Jenna had wanted to help her mum so badly but had been unable to do any more than make her last few months as comfortable as possible.

She *could* help Maria, though.

'I'll have to think about it,' she said slowly.

'Of course.' But Maria's shoulders slumped a little and she muttered something inaudible in Italian. Then she blinked away the remainder of her tears. 'Come back to the lounge for a moment. Paolo promised he would try and get home in time to meet you so you would not have to come back for another interview.'

Perhaps Paul Romano was a man of his word.

Due either to good management or luck, the surgeon was entering the front door of the house just as Maria and Jenna emerged from the kitchen and Louise was arriving at the foot of the sweeping staircase with Danielle in her arms.

For a moment nobody moved.

An eloquent snatch of time in which the situation and everybody's reactions to it were registered. The atmosphere was suddenly electric and Jenna had to take a deep breath as the swirl of undercurrents threatened to suck her under.

Louise's hold on Danielle struck a discordant note and her determination to advertise her right to be there was almost palpable. 'Look, Danielle,' she said brightly. 'Daddy's home.'

Maria's smile of welcome faded as her gaze travelled from her son to the woman holding her granddaughter. Jenna could sense the anxiety all too clearly.

But what made the air really crackle was the fact that Jenna realised instantly that Louise had no show of being the one in control. The man in that photograph had been a single dimension. The reality was overpowering.

Too good-looking, in a dark suit reminiscent of that wedding attire. The only incongruous note in the immaculate appearance came from the large, stuffed toy giraffe he was holding by one leg in the same hand as a sleek leather briefcase.

He was also charming. But the smile was well practised and did not disguise the keen assessment coming from eyes even darker than those of his daughter. His head dipped in a single nod. The kind of nod, Jenna thought with amusement, that one of his new theatre nurses might receive. She was there and, of course, she wanted the job, but she would have to prove her capability. The benefit of any doubt was not about to be bestowed.

The awkward tension broke as the briefcase was deposited beside an antique umbrella stand and Paul Romano flicked one of Danielle's silky curls with his forefinger.

'*Ciao, cara.*' He held out the giraffe, which Louise took, shaking her head.

'You spoil her, Paul. She already has an entire zoo of animals.'

Danielle took no notice of the toy. She beamed, twisting in Louise's grip to hold out her arms. 'Pa-pa!'

But her father was already turning away as his mother spoke.

'Paolo, this is Jenna Freeman.'

'Yes.' This time he held out his hand. 'Pleased to meet you, Ms Freeman.'

His English was perfect. Just enough trace of an accent in that deep voice to give it an edge that made you want to hear more. And his grip was strong. Sure. This time the eye contact was more personal. Penetrating, even. If Jenna had found the physical presence of this man overpowering, the effect of this physical contact was extremely disconcerting.

Intimidating?

Yes, but Jenna wasn't about to be intimidated. The subtle put-down of treating her as no more than a prospective employee didn't matter because Jenna had no intention of working for this man.

Not after the way he had just ignored his daughter's plea for contact. How cold a person would you have to be to resist those little arms held out like that, begging for a cuddle? And was 'Pa-pa' the only word that Ella had learned so far? Out of desperation, perhaps?

However 'difficult' Paul might find it, being left as a single father, the baby should always come first.

Yet Jenna wasn't getting the impression of a cold man from this contact. Quite the opposite, which only added to her curiosity about the dynamics of this household.

Too late, Jenna became aware that she had been staring at Paul Romano for a shade too long.

That Maria was beaming approvingly.

And that Louise had a gaze that felt like it was being filtered through the sights of a high-powered rifle.

Jenna hurriedly pulled her hand clear of Paul's touch.

That he resisted her intention to pull her hand away was hardly surprising. This was a man who was very used to being in charge. It was only for a fraction of time. A single heartbeat. Just long enough for Jenna to be startled by a flash of what could have been annoyance. Or maybe resignation.

Something that she instinctively knew was not directed at her but was a result of him being just as aware as she was of the undercurrents swirling around them.

'Come this way, Ms Freeman. I won't keep you long.'

He led her back into the room in which she had been interviewed by the grandmothers. He ignored the pages of her CV still lying on the coffee-table, but Jenna had the impression he was already familiar with its contents.

'So…Jennifer, is it?'

'I prefer Jenna.'

The smile was definitely charming. 'So do I,' Paul said. 'It sounds almost Italian.'

Then the smile faded and the gaze fixed on Jenna focussed sharply.

'You're a highly qualified nurse. Why are you applying for a job that will use virtually none of your skills?'

'I…wanted a change.'

'Why?'

Jenna took a deep breath. Talk about getting straight to the point. Fair enough, too. She'd want to know the motivation of someone she was going to employ to care for *her* child. There was no point in being less than honest.

'Six months ago I applied for a year's leave in order to care for my mother. She was terminally ill with cancer and I wanted to nurse her myself, rather than use a hospice.' Jenna did her best to keep her tone calm and professional but she couldn't help a small wobble. 'Sadly, the end came a little sooner than expected.'

The face of the man facing her softened as she spoke and when he spoke, his voice was also softer. Deeper.

'I'm *so* sorry, Jenna. I had no idea.'

Sympathy enveloped Jenna like a soft blanket. Unexpected and apparently so genuine she found, to her horror, that tears were not far away. She blinked hard. It shouldn't be a surprise that Ella's father could be this caring. After all, this was a man who had clearly loved his wife so passionately he was finding it impossible to bond with their child.

'It was the right thing to do,' he said approvingly. 'Nothing is more important than family, is it?'

'No.' Especially when it was the last of any family Jenna had.

'And you didn't want to return to your hospital position immediately?'

'I couldn't. And it also seemed like a good opportunity to make sure it *is* what I want to do. Where I want to be.'

'You have doubts?'

Doubts?

Of course Jenna had doubts about returning. Having to work in the same hospital as Simon, who would now be parading his new fiancée on his arm at every opportunity.

Paul would have understood, Jenna thought suddenly. Irrelevantly. He knew how important family was. He wouldn't have ended a relationship because a beloved, sick mother was demanding all her attention. He wouldn't have issued an ultimatum of using a hospice or losing him.

Her mother had given her a last, unintentional gift in a way. Saved her from staying in a relationship that could never have been good enough.

'I need a fresh start,' she found herself confessing. 'And I've been thinking of relocating to Christchurch. I thought I'd get more of a feel for what it would be like to live here if I took a job outside a hospital.'

Paul nodded but then frowned. 'I am a little concerned that there are time constraints on your availability,' he said, 'but, then, poor Danielle has had several changes already.' He hesitated for a moment, as though undecided whether to expand on his comment, but then his gaze dropped to the papers on the coffee-table. 'It would certainly be to our advantage to have someone with skills such as yours, even temporarily.' His nod was decisive as he looked up again. 'I want the best for Danielle. The job is yours if you want it.'

Jenna opened her mouth to say that she would have to think about it. That she had a few major reservations about a working environment that included the influence of someone like his mother-in-law. But it would hardly be politic to criticise his child's grandmother and, in any case, Jenna's momentary hesitation cost her the opportunity to say anything at all.

Paul was on his feet and the interview was over. A pager on his belt sounded as he opened the door for Jenna and he moved swiftly past Maria and Louise, who were still in the foyer, towards a phone on a small table.

Within seconds he was clearly in communication with a paediatric intensive care unit,

'What was the CBC differential?' Jenna heard him query. 'Electrolytes? Ultrasound results?'

He listened for a longer time, seemingly oblivious to everyone else standing in the foyer.

'OK. Sounds like it's only a partial obstruction but I don't want a three-day-old baby deteriorating any further. Get a consent form for Theatre signed. I'm on my way.'

With concise, well-practised movements, Paul was on the move again. He collected his briefcase, gave his mother an apologetic smile and made perfunctory farewells.

And then he was gone, as suddenly as he had arrived.

'I'm sorry,' Maria said. 'It was obviously an emergency.'

'I should probably go now as well,' Jenna said.

A grandfather clock chimed.

'Goodness, is that the time?' Louise moved towards Maria, preparing to hand over the baby. 'I have a dinner date tonight.'

Danielle and the toy giraffe were passed into Maria's arms as Jenna turned to make her farewell, and at the sight of the small girl's face, her heart lurched. Danielle was staring at the door through which her father had just disappeared.

Her eyes were swimming with tears that had just started to overflow but she was making no sound.

What kind of baby cried silently?

Lifting her gaze, Jenna had the feeling that Maria was reading her mind and a snatch of their private conversation replayed itself.

Ella needs her papa. He needs her. He just hasn't realised it yet.

And maybe he didn't realise that a cuddle was a far more precious gift than a soft toy could ever be. Ella apparently had a whole zoo of stuffed animals but how much physical contact did she get with her only remaining parent? Not much, if any, Jenna suspected. How sad was that?

Louise was putting on her coat. 'Same time tomorrow?' An answer wasn't expected. 'Goodbye, Jennifer. It was a pleasure to meet you. I hope you find the kind of job you're looking for in Christchurch.'

Jenna waited until Louise was on the other side of the door. A flash of anger at the blatant dismissal from this very unpleasant woman had been enough to put her back up.

To make her want to protect someone as

innocent as a baby from such a person. It was a feeling strong enough to shunt aside the considerable misgivings she had about taking this job.

Jenna reached out and stroked a tear from Danielle's pink cheek and then she smiled at Maria.

'How soon would you like me to start?'

CHAPTER TWO

'YOU'RE up very early today, Jenna.'

'Only because someone else decided to get up so early.' Jenna smiled at Paul but quickly dipped her head to drop a kiss among the silky black curls resting on her shoulder. To hide any expression that might reveal embarrassment.

This was the first occasion since that initial interview that she had been in Paul's company without one—or both—of the grandmothers being present. She had only been half-awake as she'd responded to the cry over the baby monitor but why hadn't she taken the time to brush her hair? And why had she just pulled on the clothes lying on the end of her bed in her haste? Her oldest jeans and a faded, racer-back T-shirt were hardly likely to impress her employer.

Ella was still in her pink, fuzzy sleepsuit. The

busy conversation of unintelligible but happy sounds she had been entertaining Jenna with on the way downstairs stopped suddenly. The baby had her thumb in her mouth as she watched her father's movements at the kitchen bench. A pot of coffee was waiting for the plunger to be depressed. Paul was busy buttering a piece of toast.

'Would you like coffee, Jenna?'

'I'll get one later, thank you. I just came down to find some more formula for Ella. We've run out in the nursery.'

'How is she today?'

'She seems much better. Her nose is still a bit runny and it was her coughing that woke me, but she's certainly a lot happier than she's been in the last couple of days. I'll keep up the paracetamol and hope her temperature stays down today.'

'Good.' Paul was slicing the toast into soldiers, one of which he offered to Ella. She accepted the gift with a coo of surprise that made both Paul and Jenna smile.

'It seems my mother was right,' Paul said. 'It *is* very reassuring to have a trained nurse caring for Danielle.'

'It's only been a mild virus.'

But the praise was warming. Or was it the unexpected bonus of Paul's company that was creating that warmth? Maybe Jenna should encourage Ella to wake early more often to try and increase the time Paul spent in the company of his daughter. So far, they very rarely saw him in the mornings and only for an hour at the most before Ella's bedtime in the evenings. A period that could easily be missed or curtailed thanks to an existing or emergency case that required the surgeon's professional expertise.

They needed more time together. A lot more.

Ella and Paul, that was. Not Paul and Jenna. Her own inclusion was desirable simply because it was necessary as a facilitator. She may have only had time to gather impressions and set an agenda so far, but her goal was crystal clear. In the space of only a week, ever since she had seen those silent tears, Ella had won her heart to the extent that the challenge now ahead of Jenna was paramount. She had six months to try and foster the bonding of a father and daughter, and success had never seemed so important.

'She likes that toast.' Smears of butter and Marmite were spread across fat pink cheeks. Any thoughts of offering to let Paul hold Ella were squashed. Imagine if he had to go and change that pristine white shirt?

Paul offered Ella another thin slice of toast, which she accepted but didn't eat. This time she held it back out, as though trying to return the gift. Paul didn't notice because he was glancing at his watch.

'It's nearly six. I'll have to run.'

'Yes. It's Wednesday.' Jenna nodded. 'It's one of your heavy theatre days, isn't it?'

An eyebrow rose. 'You know my schedule so well already?'

'Let's see.' Jenna ducked as the piece of buttery toast was waved too close to her hair. 'You operate on Mondays and Fridays as well, have outpatient clinics on Tuesday and Thursdays and you do ward rounds at least once every day. You also have umpteen departmental duties, teaching slots and, of course, way too many emergencies.'

Both of Paul's eyebrows had risen to meet the flop of dark, wavy hair on his forehead.

Jenna tried not to blush. Instead, she took advantage of the opportunity provided.

'Ella doesn't get to see that much of you,' she explained, 'and your mother always looks forward to any time you have at home.'

Maria probably didn't get that weird sensation of having swallowed a whole tribe of butterflies on anticipating Paul's company, though, did she?

A sneaking sympathy for Louise had been inevitable. It was no surprise that Danielle's other grandmother was convinced that any woman coming within an inch of Paul would want to throw herself at the man. He was, without doubt, the most physically attractive man Jenna had ever met.

Tall and dark. Lean and lithe—with the kind of dark, brooding aura that so many women found irresistible. And there was the voice. Like rich chocolate with that barely discernible but intriguing foreign inflection, not to mention the ability to switch to fluent Italian as he sometimes did with his mother. You wouldn't be a heterosexual female if you didn't respond to that attractiveness at some level.

It would wear off.

It might wear off a lot faster if she had enough time to get used to it. To file it where it belonged as simply a physical reaction to a very attractive male. Even if Jenna had been interested in Paul on a personal level—which she *wasn't*—she was focussed enough on her new goal to know that getting distracted would be a hindrance. A disaster, in fact, if Paul actually became more interested in her company than that of his daughter.

It couldn't be allowed to happen.

It *wouldn't* happen.

Things needed to be kept professional. She shouldn't have made such a personal comment. Not yet, anyway, when there were still too many large, missing pieces of the puzzle this family represented.

Jenna tried to open Ella's little fist to remove the mashed piece of toast. She also tried to sound as though Paul's timetable was purely of professional interest.

'Anything interesting on your list today?'

'Yes.' Paul drained the last of his coffee from the mug, highly relieved at the change of topic. He heard more than enough from his mother concerning the number of hours he spent at work. He certainly didn't need Danielle's nanny joining the chorus. 'A three-year-old boy, Darren Symes. He's got a Wilms' tumour.'

'Unilateral involvement?'

The surprise of having an intelligent medical question being asked in his own home was rather pleasant. There was more than one benefit in having a trained nurse as the new nanny. Paul put his coffee-mug into the sink and turned on the tap to rinse his hands.

'I'm hoping so. We haven't found any metastases but there's a question mark hanging over the state of the unaffected kidney. And, of course, I'll have to be very careful to avoid any tumour spillage.'

'How did he present?'

'Abdominal mass. GP found his blood pressure raised and a urine dipstick test detected blood. Ultrasound confirmed the nephroblastoma.' Paul dried his hands on a towel. 'I must go.'

'Good luck.'

Jenna was smiling at him. There was an understanding of the importance of what he was facing in that smile. There was also confidence that he would succeed in her tone—the wishing of luck was just a verbal token that he was unlikely to need.

He liked that.

Even more, he liked the fact that, for the first time in nearly a year, he could go to work and concentrate on what needed to be done, without having to deliberately switch off any background anxiety about what might be happening at home.

Thanks to Jenna.

An unlikely nanny. It was just as well Louise couldn't see her right now, looking like she had so recently tumbled out of bed. That cloud of dark curls falling over her shoulders, old clothes that hugged a figure far more attractive than those straight skirts and classic shirts had ever advertised and a face that obviously needed no make-up to stand out from a crowd.

Not that it would have mattered what Jenna looked like. Anyone who could have altered the atmosphere in this house to such a degree in the space of only a week would have been welcome. Paul had not seen his mother this happy in a very long time.

Curious that he was taking longer than he needed to dry his hands. That he wasn't in his usual rush to leave for work. It was this new phenomenon that was developing—the notion that dealing with the demands of his family could transcend duty and perhaps even provide a degree of pleasure.

Yes. Everybody had been happier since Jenna had arrived.

Except for Louise, of course, but if Paul was honest, the fact that his mother-in-law was not pleased only added to his current level of satisfaction. Maybe she would just give up now.

And go home.

Not that he would deny her rights as part of the extended Romano clan. Family was everything, was it not?

Yes. Paul smiled as he reached out to touch Danielle's curls.

'*Verdere piu tardi, cara.* See you later.'

He was careful to give Jenna no more than a casual glance of farewell.

Not that he should have trouble keeping the lid

on any hormonal stirring he might be experiencing. He'd had more than enough practice in the last eighteen months and the lessons of treading that particular path had been learned exceptionally well. It was Danielle and his mother who would reap the benefits of that sparkle of real intelligence, the ready smile, the soothing voice and what would, undoubtedly, be a soft touch.

He let himself out of the house and strode towards the garage. Being outside was good. Sometimes it was disconcertingly difficult to keep matters of importance in perspective when he was in the company of Danielle's new nanny.

Things may be looking brighter but he needed to tread carefully. To remember the lessons learned. But he could never have difficulty remembering, could he? Danielle was living evidence of the fallout possible from making a mistake. A mistake he would never repeat.

'What is it?'

'Twelve point three. See?' Jenna held the small blood-glucose monitor so that Maria could see the display.

'That's high, is it not?'

'We're aiming to get it stable in single figures but it's better than yesterday and you're due for your insulin anyway.' Jenna stooped to tickle Danielle, who was now crawling on the floor of Maria's bedroom. The baby giggled and held up her arms. 'Just a tick, sweetheart,' Jenna responded. 'I'm going to give Nonna her injection and take her blood pressure and then we'll all go and have proper breakfast. Are you hungry or are you still full of toast?'

Danielle flapped her arms and Maria laughed.

'It's so good having you here, Jenna.' Maria discarded the tissue she had been holding on her fingertip since the prick required for the blood-sugar test. She grimaced at the sight of the approaching syringe. 'I hate needles.'

'You know you barely feel this.'

'It's the waiting for it. The…what is the word?'

'Anticipation?'

'*Si*. The anticipation. It magnifies things.'

'Mmm.' Jenna's agreement was heartfelt. She was already thinking ahead herself. Wondering how to make best use of the time when Paul returned from work that evening.

Wishing they could see a little more of him than they did.

Be careful what you wish for!

Jenna shook off the mental warning. She could handle whatever it was going to take on this new mission of hers.

'I'll never be able to do that by myself.'

Jenna rubbed the spot, having injected the insulin, and smiled. 'I have the feeling you could manage anything you set your mind to, Maria. It can't have been easy, coming to a strange country, away from all your friends and family, to raise your son.'

Maria shrugged. 'His father wanted it so that's what we did. *His* brother went to Australia and became a big success. Roberto wanted to be the one to be successful in *Nuova Zelanda*.' The older woman pushed up her sleeve and watched Jenna wrap the blood-pressure cuff around her upper arm. 'I could not manage this.'

'You won't need to. Once we know your

blood pressure is stable on the new dose of medication, you'll only need it checked when you go to see Dr Barry.'

'Wasn't it nice of him to lend us this...what is that impossible word?'

'Sphygmomanometer,' Jenna supplied. She put the disc of the stethoscope on the crook of Maria's elbow. 'Yes, he's a lovely man. And a very good doctor, from what I could see.'

'He was very impressed that you came to the appointment with me.'

Jenna grinned. 'I think he was more impressed at your initiative in hiring a private nurse.'

Maria shook her head. 'I saw him watching you with Danielle, too. When we were leaving he said, "You've got a treasure there, Maria," and I said, "Don't I know it?"'

Jenna concentrated on the mercury level as she released the valve to hide the flush of pleasure at Maria's praise. 'Good. One-fifty on ninety. That's the same as yesterday.' She noted the pressure in a notebook along with the blood-glucose level and the dose of insulin given. 'Now, we'd better get some breakfast into you.

I don't want you getting hypoglycaemic and shaky again.'

'I feel like it's taking over my life,' Maria sighed. 'The blood prick. The injection. The right food. Tests and more tests! Watching the clock all the time to make sure that nothing is missed.'

'It'll take a while to get used to.' Jenna scooped up Danielle, who was already making a beeline for the door. Still wearing her cute pink sleep-suit and with her curls still tousled, she was irresistibly cuddly. Jenna gave her a quick kiss before turning her head to smile at Maria. 'You'll be amazed at how it becomes part of the routine in a while. Like cleaning your teeth. Once we get to know how your body reacts to the insulin and what effect things like exercise have, you should be able to get down to only two injections a day. You might even be a candidate for having a pump system that sits under your skin and administers insulin automatically.'

They were halfway along the wide, upstairs hallway now. The door to a bathroom was on the left and Jenna knew the closed door on the right belonged to Paul's bedroom. She adjusted her hold on the baby whose fuzzy sleepsuit made her feel like a living teddy bear.

What did Paul wear to sleep in?

'I do not like that idea,' Maria announced.

'Sorry?' Jenna had been dealing with an idea that was disconcertingly attractive. More than one idea, in fact. Old pyjama pants tied up with a string? Boxers? Nothing at all...?

'A pump. The needle would be there in my skin? All the time?'

'No. Actually, the whole pump system is placed under the skin. Like a pacemaker. You wouldn't feel it.' Jenna's steps slowed. 'I should get Ella dressed before we go downstairs.'

'Why bother?' Maria ruffled Ella's curls and kissed her. 'What's so wrong with having breakfast in your pyjamas?'

'Absolutely nothing.' Laughing, they moved on together towards the stairs. 'And are you sure you don't mind me wearing jeans?'

'You must wear whatever makes you happy, Jenna. I'm going to get into old clothes soon. It's such a lovely day and I wish to do some gardening.'

'But it's Wednesday.'

Maria sighed. '*Si*. So it is.'

Wednesdays weren't just one of Paul's heavy days for the operating theatre. It was also one of the weekdays that Louise chose to pay an extended visit to Hamilton Drive.

She arrived while they were still in the kitchen and the laughter Ella had generated with her own attempts to get porridge and stewed apples anywhere but into her mouth faded abruptly.

Louise bent to kiss Ella but drew back. 'What *is* that in her hair?'

'Porridge.' Jenna grinned. 'I'll go and get her cleaned up. It's time to get dressed anyway.'

'Yes.' Louise eyed the jeans Jenna was wearing as she stood up to lift Ella from the high chair. The housekeeper, Shirley, distracted her from making any comment.

'Coffee, Mrs Gibbs?'

'Yes. Black. No sugar.'

Shirley caught Jenna's gaze as she went past the back of Louise's chair. The subtle roll of the housekeeper's eyes was eloquent. As if she didn't know by now how Louise took her coffee. It was also intended to be encouraging, Jenna realised. They were all in for a long day.

One that didn't start very well.

'I'll take Danielle out for her walk,' Louise announced when Jenna brought her back downstairs.

Weather permitting, the walk was part of the routine on the days Louise visited—at least three times a week.

'She likes to show her off,' Shirley had confided to Jenna on Monday evening. 'That's why she likes to have her all dolled up in those clothes she keeps buying.'

Like the smocked dress and shiny shoes Jenna had dressed her in that morning.

'I'll bet that where she picked up her bug,' Shirley had added in a mutter.

A bug she wasn't completely over.

'I'm not sure it's a terribly good idea today,' Jenna said to Louise. 'She's been running a temperature and was coughing in the night.'

'She looks fine to me.' Louise took Ella from Jenna's arms. 'And it's a glorious day.'

Jenna couldn't contradict either statement. Ella *did* look much better, even though very little of that breakfast had made it anywhere near being swallowed. And it was a gorgeous day. One of those autumn gems that was still enough to leave the warmth of the sunshine undiminished. If they stayed at home, she would have encouraged Danielle to spend time playing outside. Was there any real difference in being taken for a walk in her stroller?

She caught Maria's gaze and the hint of alarm that Jenna, the expert, thought that her precious Ella might still be unwell. If Paul was here, Jenna thought, he would make the decision in an instant and nobody would dare argue. But if Jenna put her foot down, Louise would be very unlikely to comply. Maria would oppose her fiercely and Jenna might find herself caught in the middle of a small domestic war.

'Maybe just for a little while,' she heard herself suggesting. 'It *is* a lovely day.'

'I'll take a complete change of clothes for her.' Louise had already assumed victory. 'And a warm jacket. Get them ready, would you, please, Jennifer?'

Jenna climbed the stairs, annoyed with herself. If she had been on the familiar territory of a paediatric ward and wearing a uniform, instead of faded denim jeans, there was no way she would have hesitated to wield authority of behalf of someone as vulnerable as a baby.

But she had no authority here. Or not enough. Louise would be a formidable adversary and quite apart from the stress a disagreement with Maria could cause, her discontent had seen the last nanny sent packing. Jenna couldn't understand why Louise was accorded the power she seemed to have—it was a piece of the puzzle she had yet to find. And it was a power bestowed purely by default. Paul could remove it with a click of those long surgeon's fingers any time he chose.

So why didn't he?

Whatever the reason, if Jenna wanted to keep this job and succeed in the challenge she had set herself, she would have to choose any battles with care, and the evidence that Ella needed to be kept within the confines of her own home today was not strong enough. Even Paul had seemed happy enough that morning with the improvement in Ella's condition.

The phone call at 11.30 a.m. to pass on the information that Louise had met a friend and would be lunching at a café was no surprise but it was a worry. The easterly breeze that had sprung up was cool enough to bring Maria in from tending her basil and tomato plants.

Jenna passed on the message, adding that she hoped Louise would not have Ella sitting outside.

'Surely not!' But Maria cast an anxious glance at the clock. 'She will need to have her back in time for her sleep.'

'There's a man involved,' Shirley warned. 'You mark my words.'

Jenna had lunch in the kitchen with Maria and Shirley and Shirley's husband, John, who helped in the garden. She couldn't help casting frequent glances through the windows at scudding clouds that were now blocking the sunshine at regular intervals. By 1.30 p.m. the temperature had dropped significantly and there was still no sign of Ella's return.

'Maybe I should go and collect them in my car,' Jenna said finally. 'Even if they had lunch inside, it's a good fifteen-minute walk home and I'm really not happy about Ella being outside. It looks like it could start raining at any minute.'

'We could ring her cellphone,' Shirley suggested, 'and find out what café they're in.'

But there was no need, because they heard the sound of the front door and a moment later Louise pushed the stroller into the kitchen. A stroller that contained a wailing baby.

'She's just a bit tired,' Louise said defensively, as Maria rushed to pick up and comfort her grandaughter.

'*Dio mio!* She's cooking!'

'It got cold. She needed her jacket on.'

'Jenna?' The plea from Maria was almost desperate but Jenna was already in action, her instincts sounding a loud alarm.

She took Ella from Maria, quickly removing her outer clothing, but it did little to cool her and she was too distressed to swallow the liquid paracetamol Shirley fetched under Jenna's direction. What worried Jenna more, however, was the rate and depth at which the child was breathing.

Trying to calm her down had to be the first priority. Jenna cradled Ella in her arms, letting the small head snuggle into her shoulder. She rocked her and made soothing sounds.

'It's OK, sweetie… Everything's OK…'

Maria stood nearby, twisting her hands, her forehead creased with worry. Shirley stared at Louise between helping Jenna by fetching the medication and supplying a damp facecloth, but Louise was ignoring everybody. She helped herself to coffee and then sat down at the table.

Ella's exhausted sobbing finally ebbed and it was then that Jenna could assess what she had instinctively feared. The baby was in quite severe respiratory distress. Tiny nostrils were flaring and the muscles around her ribs retracting with the effort to breath. It was taking longer for her to breathe out than in and Jenna could now hear a faint wheeze. And the rate was high. Far too high.

'We need to take Ella to hospital,' she announced.

Maria went pale and crossed herself. Louise lifted her head sharply.

'Don't be ridiculous! She's just got a bit of a sniffle and she's tired. I'm sorry we didn't get back earlier but I met...Gerald, the man I had dinner with last week and he asked me to have lunch and...well, I could hardly refuse, could I?'

Shirley gave a soft I-told-you-so sort of snort but nobody bothered answering Louise.

'Could someone bring a car around?' Jenna asked. 'I don't want to put Ella down until I have to. Getting upset again is only going to aggravate the trouble she's having with her breathing.'

'She can't breathe? *Oh...*' Maria was hovering like a mother hen.

'What's wrong with her?' Louise demanded.

'I think she may have bronchiolitis.'

'But she seemed so much better this morning,' Maria almost wailed. 'I don't understand!'

'It often presents as a mild viral illness and the symptoms were well controlled with the paracetamol. If it had just been a cold, she wouldn't have deteriorated like this.'

'You should have known it was more than a cold. You're a nurse, aren't you?' Louise was getting to her feet. 'I hope you're not suggesting this is *my* fault.'

'What's important right now is that we get Ella to hospital so she can be monitored properly and treated if this gets any worse.'

'I'll get the car,' John offered.

'I'm coming, too,' Maria said firmly.

'So am I,' Louise snapped.

Maria paused with dramatic suddenness in her route to the door. She waved her arms in the air. '*Wait!* I must ring Paolo and let him know we're coming.'

Jenna blinked. Of course Paul should know his daughter was about to turn up in the emergency department, but what would he think if he received an alarmed call from his mother— probably in voluble Italian? Keeping everybody calm was part of her job in order to prevent the atmosphere around Ella becoming overly tense.

'Maybe Shirley could do that,' she suggested. 'That way we won't be held up.' She caught the housekeeper's gaze. 'Just let him know I'm a bit worried so we're coming in to get Ella properly checked.'

'Sure.' Shirley nodded. 'I guess they'll let me leave a message if he's busy in the operating theatre or something.'

This wasn't the way Jenna would have wanted any of them to see more of Paul Romano. She *should* have been more careful what she wished for.

Both grandmothers had been asked to wait in the relatives' waiting area and Ella was sitting on Jenna's knee in an emergency department cubicle. This was due solely to the fact that if anyone tried to remove her from Jenna's arms she immediately began to cry. With her nanny, she was calm enough to allow oxygen tubing to be held in the vicinity of her face in an attempt to bring up the level of oxygen circulating in Ella's blood.

'What's the saturation now?'

'Ninety per cent.' The paediatric registrar summoned to examine Ella flinched visibly at the unexpected, crisp query coming from behind his back. Paul had finally appeared, still dressed in his theatre scrubs and clearly impatient to find out what was going on.

Jenna was thankful she had her arms full of Ella and something she could at least pretend to be completely focussed on. She was also thankful for the conversation now going on between the consultant and the registrar, however, because it gave her a legitimate excuse to steal frequent glances at Paul.

She had never seen him looking like that.

She had never seen *anyone* looking like that.

The suggestion of weariness and, undoubtedly, anxiety for his daughter had given the surgeon an even more sombre professionalism. Or was it because they were now on his working turf?

Jenna was struck anew by this man's apparent aloofness to his child. He was acting like any other doctor might in discussing a patient. Apart from his customary flick of Ella's curls in greeting, Paul had made no attempt to comfort his sick daughter. No cuddles. No soothing words.

Was Jenna dreaming in thinking she could establish a loving connection if there was so little to build on?

The aloof, professional demeanour was at complete odds with his appearance. Too many hours under a theatre cap would have flattened those black curls. Had Paul run distracted fingers through his hair to make it look so tousled and unruly?

And the scrub suit was baggy. A deep V-neck revealed dark curls on his chest and his bare arms also had a covering of fine, very dark hair.

Jenna felt almost embarrassed. It felt like catching her employer on the way out of the shower with just a towel wrapped around his waist. Much worse than a casual chat in the kitchen of his own home. Worse even than idle curiosity about what he might wear to bed. She could feel herself flushing, as though at any moment Paul would look over to see her thoughts in a bubble over her head.

How ridiculous! As if she hadn't seen surgeons around hospitals or in wards, still wearing theatre clothing.

But she had never been involved in their private

lives, had she? Jenna felt uncomfortable. Like she was stepping over a boundary of some kind. Only she didn't know what the boundaries were.

'You'll have to admit her, then,' Paul was saying.

'Yes.'

'Provisional diagnosis?'

'Bronchiolitis. Probably RSV. We'll try a viral nasal wash to identify the causative pathogen but it won't make any difference to treatment at this stage.'

'Which is?'

'We'll give oxygen to keep the sats above ninety-two per cent. IV or nasogastric fluids at seventy five per cent maintenance and we'll keep a careful watch on her and transfer her to the paediatric ICU if she deteriorates.'

'Chest X-ray?'

'Not indicated, given that she has typical clinical features.'

Those typical clinical features that were listed in any paediatric textbook were feeling far more personal to Jenna. This was Ella in her arms. Feeling too hot, her nose rubbing against Jenna's shoulder as her head twisted in discomfort.

Feeling heavy and exhausted but forced to continue the laboured breathing.

Poor little thing. Jenna had never experienced empathy with her patients to quite this degree— even the ones that had stolen her heart. She rocked Ella gently and shifted the end of the oxygen tubing a little closer to the baby's flushed features.

Paul's attention, with startling suddenness, was transferred to Jenna. 'Why did you leave it so long to bring her in?'

The scrub suit and the body it revealed were forgotten instantly. So was any embarrassment. The unfairness of apportioning blame for Ella's condition got her back up just as instantly.

'We came as soon as I saw she was in respiratory distress.'

His gaze didn't leave hers but Jenna wasn't going to be the first to look away. To imply guilt. It wasn't easy. The weight of Ella in her arms and her concern for the child was making her feel bad enough already. Guilt was only a heartbeat away, even if it was unjustified.

'You're a paediatric nurse. I would have

expected you to pick this up well before it required urgent hospital admission.' The approval of her care of Ella that he had expressed only that morning seemed long forgotten.

He was a paediatric surgeon, for heaven's sake. He had seen how well Ella had looked at 6 a.m., stuffing a piece of toast into her mouth, and he must know just how quickly the condition of young children could deteriorate.

Then again, maybe Ella hadn't gone downhill so suddenly. There had been a period of several hours when she had been away from the observation of trained eyes.

'Mrs Gibbs had taken Ella out for a walk.'

'And you allowed this?' Paul looked astonished. And then disappointed. Jenna felt a wave of shame. He had every right to be disappointed in her. The fact that she had let herself down in a professional capacity was bad enough to make Jenna feel that disappointment like a physical blow.

She hated that Paul thought less of her. There was no point trying to defend herself or, worse, suggest that he had been in a position to make the judgement call himself.

Or to explain that there had been no clinical grounds on which to forbid the outing later in the morning and that she had been trying to act as a professional and keep her own emotions out of an already volatile mix. That she had been trying to act as a nanny and not a substitute mother.

She may have nothing to feel guilty about but from Paul's point of view, she had failed in her duty to his child. Bad enough for a nanny to be negligent but for someone who was supposed to be a senior paediatric nurse, it was inexcusable.

The bright flush in her cheeks might have gone unnoticed except that Paul paused, having flicked back the cubicle curtain. He turned once again.

'My mother tells me that Ella prefers your care to anyone else's at present.'

Jenna lifted her chin but said nothing. Did he really have to sound as though the idea that she could still do any part of her job well enough was surprising?

'She will need someone to stay in hospital with her during this admission. Day *and* night.'

Jenna nodded her agreement. She had no argument with his statement. She approved of the fact that Paul recognised its importance. Maybe he did care, just a little. Many babies were left to the care of nursing staff overnight because family circumstances made it necessary. Some even had to be separated from their family members during the day as well, but the co-operation and recovery of children who had a familiar, loving presence with them at all times was measurably better.

'I would prefer that person to be you.' The words were uttered with a certain caution. As though Paul had been persuaded—against his better judgement—that it was preferable.

Had Louise complained that she couldn't manage such a commitment, perhaps?

Was Paul concerned that the prospect of long days with a miserable baby and potentially sleep-less nights might be too much for his own mother?

Or had it been necessary to curtail the compe-tition between the two grandmothers?

Somehow, Jenna didn't think any of these ex-planations sufficed. Paul Romano was not someone who would be easily swayed from his better judgement and it would have been quite possible to arrange a roster system that allowed both Louise and Maria to share the care.

Was she being given a second chance here?

If so, she'd better make damned sure she came out with a better report card than she had just been issued with for her care of Ella. For the sake of her own self-esteem, if nothing else. Besides, she *wanted* to be the one to care for Ella.

'Of course,' Jenna said. 'I hadn't considered otherwise.'

'Good.'

His expression softened with the same fluid ease that Jenna had been startled by in that first interview. It wasn't that he was blaming her for this situation. It was more that he was understandably anxious about his daughter and perhaps he realised that he was taking it out on her. It could almost be a kind of apology.

But even if it was, why did it have the curious effect of disturbing that nest of butterflies? Of creating tension rather than relief?

'I'll see you on the ward, then.' With a nod at both Jenna and the registrar, Paul left. Presumably to start his afternoon theatre list.

The registrar eyed Jenna curiously. 'So you're a paediatric nurse?'

'Yes.'

'Working as a nanny?'

'Temporarily. I took a year's leave of absence from my job to care for my terminally ill mother. The…end came a lot sooner than we expected.'

'I'm sorry to hear that.' The registrar's glance shifted to the cubicle's curtain. The direction in which Paul had vanished. 'Must be a challenging job for you?'

'I expect it will be. I've only just started, really.' Jenna pulled a rueful face, pressing her cheek gently to the top of Ella's drowsy head. 'This isn't the best way to impress one's new boss, is it?'

'At least you'll know your way around a paediatric ward.' The registrar smiled as he saw Jenna give her charge a soft kiss. 'And you are obviously fond of wee Ella here. You're the perfect person to special this case. She's a lucky little button.'

'I just hope she gets through this without any further complications.'

'We'll make sure we keep you in long enough to be certain. Come on, I'll take you up to the ward.'

'You just have the one?'

'There's a paediatric intensive care unit, of course, but hopefully you won't need to get acquainted with that. There's also a smaller ward for acute assessment. More of an intensive observation unit.'

'So you have both medical and surgical cases on the same general ward?'

'Yes. Did you have them separated?'

'No. There's such a big overlap, isn't there? With the number of specialists that get called in from all fields, it's easier to have them all heading for the same place.'

'Exactly. We'll keep you in a private room, though. Wouldn't want RSV to spread.'

Jenna followed the registrar. They would collect the grandmothers on their way to the ward.

A ward that would have all Paul's inpatients. He would be doing rounds there probably twice a day and would be called in to assess new admissions or deal with complications at all sorts of other times.

Potentially, Ella would see much more of her father in the next day or two than she did at home.

Jenna's heart skipped a beat.

So would she.

CHAPTER THREE

ELLA still had a bottle of warm milk last thing at night to settle her for sleep and it was a time of day Jenna had already come to love.

In the past, the opportunity to sit comfortably in an armchair, cradling an infant to feed it, had always been a moment of peace in a hectic work routine. With Ella, always reluctant to surrender to sleep, it was something really special.

Jenna would find herself under the scrutiny of those serious, dark eyes that always seemed to be asking a question. One tiny, starfish hand would be on the bottle. The other would be grasping Jenna's arm and squeezing rhythmi-cally, like a kitten kneading its mother's stomach.

Tonight, with feeling unwell and all the stress of a long and frightening day, feeding time was a blessing. Ella could come out from beneath the oxygen tent overhanging her cot and be held properly.

Comforted and fed.

The hand that normally stayed in touch with the bottle was encumbered with a bulky splint and bandage, keeping the IV line protected, but the other hand held onto Jenna's arm with a new, fiercely determined grip, and the questions in the baby's eyes had an urgent quality.

'I'm here, sweetheart,' Jenna whispered. 'I'm not going anywhere.'

Ella accepted the teat of the bottle but sucked only once or twice, half-heartedly, and her little hand retained its firm grip with no release to begin the customary squeezing.

When Jenna went to remove the teat from her mouth, however, Ella's face crinkled miserably and her chest heaved with the effort of preparing to cry. She might not be hungry—probably thanks to the IV fluids she was receiving—but she needed the cuddle that went along with the routine of the feed. Jenna slipped the teat back into her mouth before the first audible squeak emerged and, at the same moment, a nurse poked her head through the doorway to their private room.

'Everything OK, Jenna?'

'Fine, thanks.'

'Is she still wheezy?'

'A bit. I think it's improved a little.'

'You'll put her back in the tent when you've finished feeding her? Her sats are probably dropping again.'

'Sure. I'll put the monitor back on as well and increase the flow if necessary.'

The nurse smiled. 'It's not often we get a trained nurse to help care for our babies.' The faint sound of a fractious child filtered in from the main ward and the nurse sighed. 'Looks like everybody wants to wake up tonight. Call me if you need anything.'

'I will.'

'And try to get some sleep yourself. That's what the bed's for, you know.'

Jenna nodded again. She should get up, she thought, and close the door properly, but she didn't want to disturb the bundle in her arms and their isolation was only semi-formal. The important issue was that Ella didn't come into close contact with any of the other inpatients.

Her gaze was already refocussed on Ella. Keeping the eye contact and trying to answer those unformed questions with reassurance.

Alone again, she rocked the baby and sang a soft song.

Surely she would fall asleep soon. It was so far past her normal bedtime and she had to be totally exhausted.

Jenna certainly was.

It had been one of the longest afternoons she had ever experienced. Even after the drawn-out trauma of the admission process and insertion of the intravenous line in Ella's hand, there had been no chance to rest. Jenna had had to liaise with the medical staff and try to keep both the grandmothers calm.

Especially Maria.

'But how will I manage without you?' Maria had been forced to wait until Louise had finally decided she would go home before she'd been able to speak to Jenna on the private matter that had clearly been weighing almost as heavily on her mind as Ella's condition. 'I can't do it! Not by myself.'

'You don't have to.' Pressing another handful of tissues into Maria's hands hadn't seemed to be sufficient, so Jenna had given her a hug. 'We'll manage together, you'll see.'

'But *how*?'

'The house is very close to the hospital. It's perfectly reasonable for you to be coming back and forth often—like you did when you fetched Ella's sleepsuit and toys. You remembered to bring everything so we'll just keep your blood-glucose kit here. I'll hide it in the drawer, see? I'll keep the insulin in the fridge and if anybody notices, I'll just say it's mine.'

'But the *pressione*. Do I need to bring the… the…?'

Jenna had shaken her head confidently. 'We won't worry about taking your blood pressure. It's only for a day or two.'

Maria had gone away looking hopeful. 'Our *segreto*,' she had murmured quite comprehensibly. 'You are an *angelo*, Jenna.'

So far it had worked. Bringing items Ella

needed had been the cover for the late afternoon treatment and she had stayed long enough to deal with the evening dose. She would be back first thing in the morning.

Which wasn't far away. It had to be well after midnight as Jenna sat singing to Ella and, at last, the dark eyes were heavily lidded. The little body was getting heavier as it relaxed.

There were no signs of increasing respiratory distress so Jenna didn't rush to put Ella back in the cot. She wanted to make absolutely sure she was not going to be roused by movement and the more deeply asleep Ella was, the better the chances.

And it was comforting. For both of them.

Jenna's song dropped to a hum. She carefully took the teat of the bottle from Ella's slack lips and put it to one side. Then she simply cuddled the baby close. Every so often, she pressed a very gentle kiss to the silky, black curls.

That was how Paul found her, a little after 1 a.m., when he paid his first visit to the room since Ella had been admitted.

It wasn't that he hadn't tried. Maria had spoken

to him on the ward much earlier but he'd been paged to the paediatric ICU to see the patient he'd operated on that morning. The registrar had informed Jenna that he'd rung for an update on his daughter's condition in the evening but he was on call and about to go into Theatre again to deal with a toddler's internal injuries after being struck by a car.

Jenna had not expected to see him until the next day. In fact, she was beginning to wonder if she would see him at all on the ward. It should have been something of a relief that she might not, given his disapproval of her care of Ella earlier but curiously a sense of disappointment was building.

She certainly hadn't expected a visit at this time of night.

Or the expression on his face that lacked even a smile of courtesy as he stood there, still wearing a very crumpled set of theatre scrubs, staring at her as she held Ella in her arms.

The hum died on her lips. She should have had Ella back in her cot by now. Under the clear, plastic tent that was keeping the oxygen levels well up in the air she breathed. How far would her saturation levels have dropped? Was Jenna about to face further—justified—disapproval of her nursing skills?

She held his gaze.

Or was he holding hers? Jenna doubted that she *could* have dragged hers away no matter how hard she tried. Paul closed the door softly behind him without breaking the eye contact and by then it had gone on a fraction too long.

Long enough for those damned butterflies to start beating a tattoo against Jenna's ribs.

Weird that she could hold the gaze of the miniature version of those eyes and respond to the unformed questions so willingly. In the subdued lighting of this quiet hospital room, Paul's eyes were black. Assessing. Asking questions that made Jenna feel the need to put herself on guard. To raise some kind of emotional sword and be ready to parry and defend herself.

And then—at the same moment he broke the eye contact—he slipped beneath that guard with an ease that took her breath away.

'I owe you an apology, Jenna,' he said.

He knew to keep his voice down but the rumble was familiar enough in any case to cause little more than a contented stretch from Ella and then a slump into a deeper unconsciousness. The tiny rasp of the baby's breathing and the faint hiss of oxygen escaping from the valve on the wall were the only sounds to fill the room.

How did Paul move so silently? Or with such grace for such a large man? With the controlled stealth of a hunting cat, he crossed the room, moved a chair to face the one Jenna was sitting on and then folded his long body to perch on its edge.

He reached out to touch Ella's curls, the way he always did in greeting.

Only this time it felt as though he was touching Jenna herself. A prickle of sensation seemed to be conducted through the baby to ripple through Jenna's entire body.

Suddenly, she was all too aware of how she must look. Probably a lot worse than she had so early that morning. Washed out. Her make-up would have worn off long since and she always went a little pale when overtired. Her clothes were grubby. Her hair a tangle of curls that hadn't seen a brush for too long. But what did it matter when it was Ella Paul had come to see?

'How is she?'

'A little better, I think,' Jenna whispered. 'This is the first real rest she's getting.' She could feel her cheeks flushing as Paul's gaze lifted to catch hers again. 'I…I should put her back in the tent.'

'I'll do it.'

His eyelids looked heavy—rather like Ella's had looked just before she'd succumbed to sleep. The lines around his eyes were deeper than normal and his chin heavily shadowed with stubble. Paul had to be even more tired than she was. She hadn't been on her feet since before 6 a.m., dealing with major surgery and emergencies. But he wasn't going to sit back and watch what needed to be done now. His hands slid beneath Ella to lift her gently.

A task that necessitated a physical contact that was astonishingly disturbing.

He's just a parent, Jenna reminded herself with a touch of panic. You've handed sleeping infants to their parents a thousand times. Times when she hadn't even been conscious of the brush of a hand against the skin of her arms.

Or fingertips that reached her breast.

Right now she was conscious of nothing else, but fortunately Paul seemed unaware of the small, shocked intake of her breath. He took his daughter with all the care he might extend to a particularly intricate surgical technique, managed to transfer her to the cot without getting the IV line tangled and then laid her on the soft mattress and slipped his hands free so slowly Jenna had to keep holding her breath.

She could feel the slow slide of those hands on her own back.

She *wanted* to feel them.

A delicious dragging sensation that would leave an aching want in its wake.

Jenna had to move. Reaching for the oxygen saturation probe that clipped to Ella's foot was the ideal way to shake this appalling reaction she was experiencing.

One that surely was only there because she was so tired. And because of the odd intimacy of this dim room, shut away from the rest of the ward, where conversation was taking place in whispers. Or was it more because of the way Paul had destroyed her ready defences by saying he owed her an apology?

Had he been referring to the blame he had bestowed in the emergency department? And was that hushed statement the extent of the apology?

Maybe not.

Paul sat down again on the upright spare chair and this time he sat on it properly, as though he intended to stay there. Jenna returned to the armchair. She pulled her feet up and curled into its soft cushion, wrapping her arms around her legs. A physical defence, perhaps? Was it simply exhaustion making her feel oddly vulnerable?

She also kept her gaze on the small screen that was showing the percentage level of oxygen circulating in Ella's blood as the figures climbed slowly to an acceptable range.

Eighty-four…eighty-six…ninety-two…ninety-five…

Jenna could breathe again.

Almost.

Keeping his voice down gave Paul's words a

seductive edge that made it difficult to concentrate on what he was saying.

'My mother tells me you tried to stop Louise
taking Danielle out today.'

'I…' She hadn't tried hard enough, had she?

Paul misinterpreted her hesitation. 'She is not
always the easiest person to negotiate with. I
know this.'

He lifted a hand—a casual but eloquent gesture
that suggested Louise's faults might be a trial but
they were something they all had to accept.

'Thank you for bringing Danielle into the
hospital. It was where she needed to be.'

'Not for long, I hope.'

'No.' Paul cast a glance at the nearby cot. 'I
shouldn't imagine so.' He rose to his feet and
then stooped to pick up a toy that had fallen from
the cot. A grey, beany rabbit with overly long
limbs and fluffy white feet and ears.

'Poor Letto,' Paul murmured. 'Getting all dusty.'

'That's her favourite toy,' Jenna said. For some
reason she wanted to try and draw out the conversation. 'Is Letto an Italian name?'

Paul's nod was absent-minded. 'Short for

coniglietto. Means rabbit. Or bunny.' He dropped the toy near Ella's feet. 'I will be back in the morning. I will bring my mother and you will be able to have a break.'

'I'm happy to stay with Ella.' Mind you, a long, hot shower might be very welcome by then.

She was getting that assessing look again but this time it didn't seem threatening.

'My mother has become very fond of you already, Jenna,' Paul said evenly. 'So has Danielle, by all accounts. You are doing well.'

The praise was sincere. Just as she had known the first time he'd looked at her that she would have to earn a good impression, she knew now that praise was not bestowed prematurely.

The smile that touched his lips was weary but it was also sincere. Not part of that automatic charm that was as much a part of Paul Romano as his dark eyes and olive skin. It made the corners of his eyes crinkle and softened the hard line of that determined jaw.

Jenna couldn't help smiling back.

A smile that returned, unconsciously, a little while later as Jenna finally dozed in her chair.

* * *

Any lack of seeing Ella's father on the day of her admission was shaping up to be made up for on the following day when Paul arrived in the room at 7.30 a.m.

The visit was perfectly timed as far as Jenna and Maria were concerned. Maria's blood test and insulin dose had been long since dealt with and Jenna was now seated in the armchair again, this time with Ella showing far more enthusiasm for her bottle of milk.

Maria was bustling about. Supplies from home had been emptied onto the bed from the cavernous black bag she liked to carry and she was now sorting baby clothes and putting the ones that needed washing back into the bag. The task was abandoned the instant her son walked through the door.

'Paolo!' she cried with delight. Her outstretched hands commanded a response but Jenna couldn't detect any hesitation on Paul's part to walk into them. You would have thought these two hadn't seen each other for a week, given the affectionate greeting, as Paul bent his head to kiss Maria on both cheeks. His own cheeks were then patted firmly enough to raise their colour but Paul was smiling.

'You are well, Maria? You look well.'

'I am fine, Paolo. You were so late last night—I was worried about you!'

'I came to visit Danielle. And then I had another call. It was so late by then, I decided to sleep here.'

He can't have had more than a couple of hours' sleep, Jenna realised. Why didn't he look as jaded and dishevelled as she was feeling? He was wearing the dark suit she remembered from her first meeting with him. With a crisp, white shirt and a carefully knotted tie. Consultant's clothes. Funny that she had been far more impressed when he had been wearing those crumpled scrubs.

'Danielle is looking so much better, yes?' Maria was turning her son towards the armchair, but his first glance was towards Jenna rather than his daughter. A glance that lingered just long enough to reflect the smile of greeting.

A smile that was just as warm as the one she had received so late last night. The kind that had haunted those half-dreams in her attempts to catch some sleep during the night.

Some neural circuit had been reinforced through repetition and its effect was instantaneous. Jenna could feel her heart rate increase and the extra blood flow that chased away fatigue made every cell in her body come a little bit more alive.

Jenna had time to come to the conclusion that the sensation was very pleasant after Paul's gaze dropped to watch Ella sucking on her bottle. Matching dark eyes were watching the surgeon's every move as he stepped closer to touch her curls, and she released the teat of the bottle with a noisy gurgle to smile at her father. Ella let go of the bottle to wave a hand and Jenna shifted the weight of the baby as she smiled at Paul.

'Would you like to hold her?'

He didn't visibly flinch or step back but Jenna could sense the sudden wariness as clearly as if he had. Her suggestion was being bounced back at her, like a kind of shock wave.

Paul avoided her gaze and Jenna felt suddenly weary again.

You idiot, she told herself. *Don't push it!*

'I can't stop,' Paul said smoothly. 'We had a lot of admissions yesterday and I'm late for a huge ward round. I'll be back later.' He flicked one of Ella's curls again. 'Finish your breakfast, *cara*.'

His fingertips brushed Jenna's bare arm but the touch felt like a warning. The boundaries were becoming clearer and Jenna was forced to step back. She turned to Maria.

'Would you like to hold her, Nonna?'

'Yes, yes—of course!'

The day-shift nurse, Beth, appeared in the doorway as Jenna handed Ella to Maria.

'Dr Romano? They're bringing Darren down from ICU now. You said you wanted to know.'

'Yes, thank you. I'll go and meet them.'

'And, Jenna? The bathroom's free if you'd like a shower. I can come and look after Ella.'

'*I* am looking after Ella,' Maria announced.

'OK.' Beth smiled. 'Just ring the bell if you need anything. Come with me, Jenna. I'll find you a towel and show you where everything is.'

When Jenna emerged from the bathroom fifteen minutes later, refreshed and dressed in the clean clothes Maria had brought from the flat, she felt ready for anything.

Except for what she saw in the private room next to Ella's.

There was quite a crowd of people around the bed. Nursing staff and junior doctors were arranging personal belongings and enough monitoring equipment to suggest that this patient required a high level of care. The parents of the patient were looking rather lost, standing back and watching the activity, but the small boy on the bed was looking surprisingly happy. He had a huge grin on his face, in fact, clearly due to the toy that was being waggled above his head and apparently making funny noises.

What brought Jenna to a startled halt and made her jaw drop was that the person holding the fluffy toy and making the noises was the patient's consultant surgeon.

None other than Paul Romano.

The man who, for some unidentified reason, couldn't even play with his own daughter!

Beth was back in Ella's room, changing the sheets on the cot.

'Who's next door?' Jenna asked. 'The patient from ICU?'

'Yes. That's Darren.' Jenna was already accepted as an honorary staff member by these fellow paediatric nurses and the normal rules of confidentiality were ignored. 'Dr Romano did a nephrectomy on him yesterday morning for a Wilms' tumour. They thought the remaining kidney was going to fail, but he's bouncing back.'

'Cute kid.' Jenna was still trying to assimilate the sight of Paul entertaining the child. It was so out of character for the man she'd thought she was getting to know. And it was disturbing. Compared to how he was with a child who was a comparative stranger, he was cold with his own child. Jenna didn't like that.

She hadn't needed to see him interacting with one of his patients to know he was capable of affection. He clearly loved his mother. Why on earth couldn't he love his daughter? It obviously wasn't that he didn't know how so it had to be a deliberate choice not to interact with Ella so closely.

Maybe she was wrong in accepting those

boundaries. Maybe she should have pushed harder, in fact. Just shoved his daughter into his arms, instead of asking for acquiescence.

'He does look like a cutie.' Beth bundled up the used linen from the cot. 'We'll special him for a day or two but I don't expect he'll be any problem.' She smiled at Ella who was being bounced gently on Maria's knee. 'He's a lucky boy, having your daddy to look after him. Now, are you ready for a clean nappy, chicken?'

'I can do that,' Jenna offered.

'That would be great. The team will be in to see you soon on their rounds, which I'd better get ready for. With Ella feeding as well as she did this morning, they'll probably take that IV line out. Her breathing sounds a bit better, too.'

'Maybe they'll let us go home today.'

Beth chuckled. 'Don't bet on it. They'll want a completely clean slate before they discharge Dr Romano's child. I'd put money on you having at least one more night here.'

The medical consultant confirmed Beth's opinion when he came to do his rounds.

'I'm happy for us to go to oral hydration but I

want her temperature right down and her chest clear before we let you go. Maybe tomorrow for discharge.'

Jenna was happy with the decision, not just because the responsibility for Ella was being shared with experts. Being back on such familiar territory was a reminder of how much she missed the job she was trained to do.

It didn't matter that it was a strange hospital. What went on inside it was the same and she was a part of this world. The ready acceptance by staff she had encountered made her feel completely at home. It was even easy to find the staff cafeteria at lunchtime when Louise was taking her turn to look after Ella and Maria had gone home for a break.

Jenna's friend, Anne, was waiting for her outside the cafeteria door.

'Are you sure you've got time for lunch?' Jenna queried. 'It sounded like you were being run off your feet in ED when I rang.'

'We are. It was a mistake to start day shifts. I think I'll go back to nights.'

'How are Dave and the kids coping?'

'I'm only doing two shifts a week so far. Let's grab some food and then we'll have time to talk. It's so good to see you.'

'I'm sorry I haven't been to visit. You were working on the only nights I've had off so far.'

'Well, I've got half an hour now and I'm hanging out to hear about you and Dr Romantico.'

'Dr *who*?'

'No, no!' Anne laughed. 'Not Dr Who! Good grief, Dave's even got the kids watching his DVD collection now. No, I'm talking about your new boss. Paulo Romantico.'

Both women leaned over the counter to choose from the triangular plastic packages containing a variety of sandwiches.

'You're the envy of every nurse in ED, you know,' Anne continued. '*Living* with him!'

'That's not what you've been telling people, is it?' Jenna widened her eyes in mock horror but the thought that even light-hearted gossip could get back to Paul was a worry.

If he was still so much in love with his dead

wife that he couldn't bond with his daughter, he wouldn't appreciate the idea that anyone thought he might have chosen a replacement as a live-in companion. And if Louise heard, Jenna would be gone from her position in a flash.

'I'm not living *with* him, as you well know, Anne. I have a self-contained flat, which is really nice. You should come and see it. I've got a separate entrance so it shouldn't be a problem to have visitors, and I'm sure Maria wouldn't mind.' Jenna chose a bottle of water and a banana to complete her meal. 'Maria's lovely. She'd probably insist on making you a lasagne or spaghetti Alfredo or something. She teaches Italian cooking, did you know that?'

'No.' And Anne clearly wasn't going to be distracted by Jenna's babbling. 'He is gorgeous, though, isn't he? I couldn't believe it when you told me who you were going to be working for.'

Jenna thought about that smile. That look of total focus that eyes as dark as sin were capable of bestowing.

'Oh, yes,' she murmured. 'He's gorgeous, all right.'

'Aha!' Anne led the way to a corner table. 'So you do fancy him, then? Hooray! It's about time something good happened in your love life.'

'*Nothing* is happening!' Jenna cast a quick glance at the nearby tables, hoping no one would be overhearing this conversation. Hospital grapevines were more lush than any jungle plants.

'But it *could*,' Anne said encouragingly. 'And why not? You're young, single and gorgeous. He's...not so young but gorgeous enough to make up for it.'

'His last nanny was sacked because she fancied him.'

'Really?'

Jenna shrugged. 'The official reason is that she had a row with Louise but that was the reason for the row as far as I know.'

'Who's Louise?'

'Paul's mother-in-law. Hey, did you know his wife? Gwendolyn?'

'I met her once at a barbecue. That was enough.' Anne made a face as she opened her sandwich package. 'She worked in Theatre.'

'I know.' Jenna peeled the seal from her water

bottle. 'Louise told me. A *theatre* nurse, she said, as though it was the pinnacle of any nurse's career aspirations. Far superior to being a paediatric or ED nurse, that's for sure.'

'She used to supply her own hats, apparently. Cute ones with pictures on them like puppies or ducks. She probably had designer scrub suits as well.'

Jenna could believe it. 'She could have been a model, according to Louise. Or a concert pianist. Or an Olympic horserider. She only chose to be a nurse because she was such a caring person.'

Anne almost choked on her mouthful of food. Having swallowed hastily, she snorted. 'She cared about herself. Not that I'm going to speak ill of the dead or anything, but I have to say she wasn't very popular around here.' Anne grinned. 'Took after her mother, by the sound of it. Is she driving you nuts, telling you how perfect Gwennie was?'

'Paul adored her.'

'Let me guess—Louise told you this?'

'I think it's true. Maria thinks that's why he can't bring himself to love Ella.'

'He doesn't love Ella?'

'He avoids having anything much to do with her.'

'But he loves kids. It's one of the things that makes him so gorgeous. I've seen him in ED once or twice and he's great with children.'

Jenna nodded. She had seen that for herself, that very morning.

'Is Ella a difficult kid?'

'No way. She's adorable. I can't understand it.'

'Neither can I.' Anne was looking fascinated. 'He's Italian. They're supposed to be totally into family stuff.'

'He loves his mother. Maybe the grandmothers are right. He misses the perfect Gwendolyn too much to be able to bear the company of her child.'

'No.' Anne was staring thoughtfully at her friend. 'I don't buy that. I mean, I adore Dave in spite of the Dr Who DVDs and if he dropped dead, I'd be hanging onto every memory. Especially the living ones. His kids…*our* kids.'

'That's what I thought, too. It's a mystery.'

'Maybe not.' Anne reached for her second sandwich. 'Maybe he didn't want to have children. Maybe their marriage wasn't so perfect and she got pregnant to try and solder it together and now he's left with a kid to raise and a mother-in-law who won't go home and he can't enjoy being single again.'

Jenna didn't want to believe that Paul could be that distant. Uncaring. But, in a way, it had a ring of truth. He had such a strong sense of duty. It was caring, but without the most important factor. The emotional involvement. And no matter what the marriage had been like, Ella was his child.

'I think he's just buried his grief in his work so successfully he doesn't want to rock the boat.' If she could persuade Anne, maybe she could hang onto the belief herself. 'He just needs time and enough contact with Ella. Nobody could resist her if they spent enough time with her.'

'Time!' Anne shot a glance at her watch and groaned. 'How did that half-hour go so fast? I've got to go.'

'Me, too.' Jenna collected the wrappers. 'I'll come and see you on my next night off. You'll be home if you're still on days, anyway.'

'Yes. Come for dinner. You'll have to put up with Dave and boys but we can shoo them off to watch TV or something after dinner.'

'I'll look forward to it. A dose of "normal" family would be great.'

Anne frowned as they reached the corridor. 'Are you not enjoying this job, then? You could always resign, you know. ED is *so* short-staffed. Paeds probably is as well. You'd get a job like a shot.'

'No.' Jenna shook her head as their paths separated. 'I couldn't do that.'

Jenna found herself quickening her pace on her way back to the ward, surprised at how the thought of abandoning Ella could have struck such a nerve.

Lost in her thoughts, she veered into Ella's room a few minutes later without looking and walked straight into the figure that was coming out.

She didn't need to look up to know that the hands gripping her arms to steady her belonged to Paul. Her body told her that instantly, with a curious tingling that only intensified when she looked up.

'Sorry,' she muttered. 'I wasn't looking.'

Another fault a good nurse would not have, but Paul sounded almost amused.

'My fault entirely,' he said. 'I was in too much of a hurry. You are all right?'

Jenna nodded. She didn't need his hands to steady her now but he was blocking the doorway. He would need to let go so that she could step backwards.

'Is that you, Jennifer?' Louise's voice came from behind Paul. 'Good. I've been waiting for you to get back. I'm going to be late for my appointment with my hairdresser if I don't leave now.'

Paul had kept eye contact with Jenna as Louise had been speaking and there was a message there. We have to put up with this difficult woman, it suggested, for Ella's sake. She *is* her grandmother.

And more. The hint of a smile said that they might have to put up with it but they didn't have to *like* it.

It was a moment of real connection. Just a split second, but it was enough for something fundamental to change. And then Paul let go of Jenna and they both stepped back simultaneously and the connection was broken.

Well broken. Jenna could see Ella staring at her father. She was holding her treasured grey bunny by its ear but even as Jenna caught sight of her, she let the toy drop to the floor.

Poor Letto.

No. Poor Ella. Anyone could see she wanted her father. Would it have been such a big ask for him to have spent a few minutes alone with his daughter so Louise could have gone to her appointment without waiting for Jenna's return?

Jenna couldn't help staring at Paul as he moved to pass her.

'Excuse me.' His tone was clipped now. Dismissive. 'I've got a patient I have to visit.'

Which was probably true, but it didn't excuse all the other opportunities Paul had had—even in the short period of time Jenna had been involved in this family.

Maybe that was what was so strange. As far as Jenna was aware, Paul never spent time alone with Ella. Or held her. Or played with her by waggling fluffy toys to make her laugh. He only saw her when she was in the care of others because she was *always* in the care of others.

A kind of indignation on Ella's behalf surfaced that Paul could treat his patients with more warmth than his own child.

It was more than unjust. It was wrong.

Jenna stared thoughtfully at Paul's back for a moment as he headed further into the ward.

Time wasn't all that was needed, was it? Ten months should have more than long enough. The shock of having his daughter sick enough to be admitted to hospital should have been enough to make him realise what he stood to lose.

Forcing the issue wasn't going to be the way forward. Too easy for Paul to take shelter behind the demands of his career. But stepping obediently back from the barriers she sensed wasn't the way to go either.

There had to be another way to bridge the gap. And Jenna had to be the perfect person to build that bridge. On the one hand, she understood and respected Paul's devotion to his work. On the other, she already loved his daughter.

And the material for building that bridge might have just made itself apparent in that moment in the doorway.

That flash of connection.

Would she be playing with fire to even consider getting closer to Paul Romano on a personal basis?

Of course she would.

Would it be worth it, for Ella's sake?

The forlorn cry as Louise put the baby back into her cot and turned to collect her handbag was like an answer in itself.

Of course it would.

CHAPTER FOUR

THE child collapsed without warning.

One moment the ten-year-old girl was walking down the ward corridor, passing Ella's room, and the next she had crumpled gracefully to the floor.

Paul was at the nurses' station at the other end of the corridor, and for just a split second he was stunned—his brain trying to register the significance of what he was seeing.

Jenna reacted faster. By the time Paul's body was gathering the momentum to run, she was crouched over the child, shaking her gently and calling for a response.

There didn't appear to be any.

Paul turned his head swiftly to see who was available but the station was empty. The nursing staff were busy on their last round of the evening, dispensing medication and trying to settle children for the night. Junior medical staff were either occupied elsewhere or had gone home.

Jenna had tilted the child's head back now and lifted her chin to open the airway. He could see the automatic position she adopted, leaning down with her cheek close to the girl's face, with a hand resting lightly on her abdomen to check for respirations.

She knew what she was doing.

Was it just a syncopal episode? A faint that would resolve itself within seconds? He had seen the girl earlier, spoken to her even, when she'd been in the playroom with her mother and younger brother who had been playing with one of Paul's patients. What was her name?

Jessica. She'd been limping badly. Rheumatic fever, that's what she'd been admitted for—a complication from an untreated streptococcal infection of her throat. She had migratory polyarthritis, giving her painful joints. And hadn't her mother said something else?

Carditis.

Paul didn't need to see how Jenna's head dipped, her mouth covering the child's to deliver a breath, to know how serious this was. He'd already reached that conclusion from the knowledge that the infection Jessica had was affecting her heart and could cause an arrhythmia.

Neither did he need to hear Jenna's clear call.

'Help! I need some help here!'

He veered into the treatment room at a run, grabbing the crash cart. It hit the doorframe with a metallic clang as he swivelled to jab a finger at the cardiac arrest button on the wall.

Jenna had started chest compressions by the time he got to them, which had to be only thirty seconds since the collapse. He threw her a bag mask, which Jenna picked up and held securely over the girl's face, squeezing the bag to deliver another breath.

'Oxygen?' she queried.

'Not on the cart. We'll send someone for a portable in a tick. Carry on—you're doing a great job.'

Paul plugged the cable for the leads into the defibrillator and unzipped the side pouch to pull out the package containing the pads. No paddles now, with the new CPR protocols in place. Aware of what Jenna was doing, he could tell she was also up with the play.

Thirty compressions to two breaths. For all age groups. Carefully timed and delivered breaths to avoid hyperventilation, which could cause poor cerebral perfusion and blood flow.

She looked calm. The tension was there because she knew exactly how serious this situation was but she was perfectly confident that she was doing what she should be doing. Paul liked that. It was precisely the way he operated himself.

Pounding feet along the corridor advertised the arrival of more nursing staff.

'Shall I take over compressions?' one asked.

'No.' Paul was attaching the sticky pads to Jessica's chest. 'Jenna knows what she's doing.'

'It was a sudden collapse,' Jenna said. 'No evidence of prior symptoms. She'd just said hello to me as she went past the door.'

'I know. I saw it.'

'What's she in for? Does she have a heart condition?'

'Rheumatic fever. Myocarditis.'

'So this is probably arrhythmic?"

'Yes.' The pattern on the screen was settling. A wild squiggle incompatible with a functioning heart.

'VF,' Jenna breathed.

'Clear!' Paul ordered. He was adjusting the joule setting on the life pack. A ten-year-old child, approximately thirty kilograms. No, this girl was slight for her age. More like twenty-five. Five joules per kilo. First and subsequent shocks at one hundred and twenty-five joules, then.

'Stay clear,' he instructed after delivery of the first shock, already recharging.

Jenna's recommencement of CPR was so instant and so smooth, following delivery of the third shock, it was like an extension of the protocol rolling through Paul's mind.

She was good. Very good.

Where was the arrest team? He needed expert help to intubate and gain intravenous access for drug therapy. He didn't know the level of skill available among the night staff gathering around them.

'Kendra?' Paul caught the gaze of the most senior nurse present. 'How are you on IVs?'

The nurse's jaw dropped. 'I haven't done one for ages!'

'Jenna?' The word was a snap.

'Confident,' she replied with equal succinctness.

'Right. Kendra, take over compressions, please. Someone get a portable oxygen cylinder. Someone else can see where that arrest team is. Jenna? See if you can get IV access, please. I'm going to intubate.'

A further, single shock was delivered after two more minutes of CPR. For just a few seconds a normal rhythm appeared on the screen and then it degenerated again into the fatal squiggle.

'Jenna?'

'I'm in.'

And she was. The IV cannula was in the crook of Jessica's elbow, the luer plug already screwed on. Jenna was taping it down, a syringe and ampoule of saline ready on the floor beside her to check and flush the line.

'Forget the flush,' Paul instructed. 'Draw me up 1.2 mils of adrenaline.'

Paul inserted the endotracheal tube while Jenna was drawing up the first dose of medication. She held the ampoule for him to check and was following directions to inject the medication when the cardiac arrest team arrived.

A doctor stared at Jenna. 'Who the hell is that?'

'She's a paediatric nurse.' Paul's tone made it clear that he took responsibility for any irregularity and he was not going to waste time right now defending himself. 'A very good one.'

Nevertheless, Jenna was rightly shunted aside as the more qualified medics took over. Amiodarone, another anti-arrhythmic drug, was given. More CPR. Another shock. And then, finally, a normal sinus rhythm appeared. And held.

'We need a stretcher,' someone said. 'Or a bed. Let's get this girl up to Intensive Care.'

Paul went with them—a small, travelling circus of personnel and equipment. Still tense but triumphant. The resuscitation had been successful.

Paul couldn't wait to get back to the ward and let Jenna know just how successful. An hour after her collapse Jessica was sitting up in bed in the paediatric intensive care unit, surrounded by monitoring equipment and consultants, wondering what all the fuss was about.

Her parents had been summoned but hadn't arrived until after their daughter had regained consciousness. They, too, had been bewildered but happy to accept that the danger was over for the moment and with careful watching, there was every chance that this frightening episode had been a one-off complication of an illness that was being appropriately treated.

Disappointingly, Jenna was not in Danielle's room.

Maria sat by the cot, knitting needles clicking in time with the hum of a lullaby that didn't appear necessary because Danielle was sound asleep.

No IV line or oxygen tent now. Keeping her in tonight was merely a formality. She would be checked on the paediatricians' round in the morning and Paul fully expected her to be discharged.

'Maria? Where's Jenna?'

Maria answered him in the language he'd automatically used—the native Italian that had always been spoken at home until his father had died.

'I sent her to make herself a cup of tea. She looked tired, poor angel.'

Hardly surprising. The aftermath of the kind of adrenaline rush an arrest scenario could generate was often a sharp downward trajectory. Especially when you didn't get the chance to talk it over with someone. To debrief. He'd had an hour of interacting with his colleagues as they'd instituted new management for Jessica's case and he still felt drained himself.

'She'll be back soon. Sit, Paolo. Talk to your mother for once.'

Paul received a keen glance when he didn't respond immediately but then Maria clucked her tongue and her mouth twitched. 'I expect she's in the kitchen.'

A moment of very uncharacteristic indecision assailed Paul. His mother was reading too much into his desire to see Jenna. When it came to his reaction to any new woman that swam into his orbit, her antennae were as sharply tuned as Louise's.

The difference was, Maria wanted happiness for her loved ones. She was not on a mission to ensure he worshipped a ghost for the rest of his life. A mission that was so focussed he didn't even have to show interest himself. The last poor girl that had been employed to help care for Danielle had made the mistake of making *her* interest obvious, and Louise had swooped like an eagle onto an unsuspecting *coniglietto*.

It was just as well he had learned to keep his own feelings so well hidden. There was no need for Louise to know that Gwendolyn's ghost was one that Paul would have difficulty respecting, let alone anything implying more reverence.

And life at home was much more pleasant. Paul wasn't about to risk the new status quo by allowing Jenna to become anything other than the nanny.

Except…that there was a new respect in that quarter. Was it because of the way she had taken on board with such dignity that unfair accusation that she had failed in her duty of care to Danielle? That she had been able to accept an apology without making him pay in some way?

Or was it a professional respect due to the manner in which she had handled Jessica's sudden collapse? He would certainly trust her from now on. He would be happy to have her on his team in the hospital. He was lucky that she had chosen to care for Danielle. Another good reason to make sure he didn't give Louise any ammunition.

Yes. His mother might have it wrong but it would make him happy at this moment to see Jenna.

To pass on the news about Jessica and see those hazel eyes light up with pleasure. Her lips curve into one of those delicious smiles usually reserved for others—like his mother or Danielle.

'Go!' Maria commanded, pointing a knitting needle towards the door. 'Tell Jenna I am happy. She doesn't need to hurry back.'

So Paul went, amusement vying with a slight annoyance. He was thirty-six, for heaven's sake! He had long since given up calling his mother 'Mama' but his affection for her could still persuade him to obey her commands a little too readily at times.

Sure enough, Jenna was alone in the staff kitchen.

She stood at the bench, lifting a teabag from a steaming mug. She turned at the sound of Paul's entrance and her reaction was startling, to say the least.

The teabag fell from the spoon to land on the stainless-steel bench with a splat, but Jenna didn't notice. Her eyes were fixed on Paul and there was just enough light from the fluorescent ceiling strip to see the way her pupils widened.

Why would someone as calm and collected in a life-and-death situation involving a child be so disturbed by his, albeit unexpected, entrance?

A question that was no less intriguing because Paul had a perfectly good idea of the reason.

He was experiencing a similar kick in his own gut.

He'd noticed it earlier today—during that little mix-up at the doorway to Danielle's room. After she had bumped into him with enough force to flatten her breasts against his chest. He'd held her arms, both to curtail the contact before Louise could get the wrong idea and to steady her. Inevitable that they should both share the same distaste for the tone of voice Louise had chosen to issue orders to Danielle's nanny.

But it had been more than a simple recognition of another's viewpoint.

It had been an understanding.

The kind that needed a chemical pathway to travel along.

The kind of chemistry that only came when attraction was mutual.

No! Don't go there!

The whisper was superfluous. Paul had no intention of exploring that pathway. It was, however, rather pleasant to know that it was there. It added considerably to the pleasure he was already experiencing.

'I just wanted to let you know that Jessica is fine,' he told Jenna. 'Quite stable. She's conscious.'

'Oh!' Jenna's face flushed and her eyes positively lit up, the joy accentuating tiny gold flecks in her irises that Paul hadn't previously noticed. But, then, he hadn't been this close to her before, had he? Not since his opinion of this woman had undergone a new definition anyway. Why *had* he stepped quite this close?

'That's fabulous,' Jenna was saying. 'I was so worried.'

'Her parents wanted me to pass on their thanks. I told them that your admirably prompt response was a major factor in averting a much more serious situation.'

Jenna ducked her head. 'Hardly!' She noticed the teabag lying on the bench and reached to pick it up. 'You were only a couple of seconds behind me and I didn't even know where the crash cart was kept.'

So she was modest about her talents. Paul liked that.

'But it was several minutes before the arrest team arrived. The staff on tonight were obviously all less experienced than you.' His gaze tore themselves away from the sight of her fingers squeezing the remaining moisture from the teabag before dropping it into the rubbish bin.

The tilt of her head as she leaned towards the bin revealed the faint movement of her carotid pulse. It was beating just a little faster than normal but you would expect an increase in heart rate to go with those dilated pupils. Disconcertingly, Paul could feel his own heart rate speeding up to match.

Even more disconcerting was the urge he had to sweep the tendrils of her long, dark hair aside properly so that he could feel the beat of that pulse with his lips. His tongue…

His line of vision was as palpable as any touch. Jenna could *feel* him staring at her neck.

Dear lord, was he thinking of *kissing* her?

It wouldn't be the first time a kiss had been stolen in a deserted ward kitchen late in an evening. Always illicit, thanks to the setting, but some were far more illicit than others.

The heat from the teabag was still intense enough to scald her fingers but Jenna held onto it as a means of buying just a brief flash of time.

She could *not* kiss Paul Romano, despite the affirmative messages now pulsing from every nerve ending in her body.

He was her employer.

No. Strictly speaking, Maria was Jenna's official employer but Paul was Ella's father.

Ella.

The name was enough to bring Jenna to her senses. That little girl needed her. So did Maria. So did Paul, although he might not realise it. How stupid—selfish—would it be to jeopardise what she stood to achieve for the sake of a few seconds of physical pleasure.

And Jenna needed the success of this mission herself. For the satisfaction of feeling she might have contributed to sorting out a small, troubled corner of the world. A kind of catharsis to cancel out the sadness of the last few months of her life. A stepping stone to a new and more positive future.

The teabag landed amidst a few empty yoghurt cartons and some snack-bar wrappers. Jenna kept her gaze carefully away from Paul's. It would be a fatal mistake to get locked into eye contact right now.

'Would…would you like a cup of tea?'

'*Grazie.*' Paul stepped back as Jenna straightened and turned. The lapse into Italian and his faintly startled blink made Jenna wonder if he'd even realised how close he had been standing to her. Or how intense his stare had been.

She filled another mug with boiling water and dropped a fresh teabag into it.

'Milk? Sugar?' The mundane could be a blessing, she decided. Nerve endings were settling now. She had only imagined his intention to kiss her. Why on earth would Paul be attracted at all? His adored wife had been a willowy blonde with strikingly defined features and an air of sophistication Jenna wouldn't even want to emulate. She couldn't be more different.

'No sugar. Just milk.'

Jenna handed over the hot drink and debated whether to cross the room to sit at the small, Formica-topped table. No. That would be inviting Paul to sit with her and might suggest that she wanted to encourage his attentions.

And she didn't.

Well, she did to some extent but it was going to be a fine line to travel, trying to create a relationship that would allow enough trust to further her mission without tipping over into intimacy.

It couldn't be rushed. Better to try and stay professional. Jenna leaned back against the bench. She held her mug with both hands and hopefully gave every impression that she was enjoying a drink that was, in fact, tastelessly burning her mouth.

Paul copied her stance, one hip resting against

the edge of the bench and a relaxed line to his body that was at odds with the way he was looking at her over the rim of his mug.

Oh, help!

Keep it professional, she reminded herself.

'How's Darren?' Jenna heard herself asking with a touch of desperation. 'The little boy next door to Ella,' she added hurriedly. 'With the Wilms' tumour?'

Paul inclined his head. 'Yes. I know who Darren is.' His lips curved just enough to suggest a smile being repressed. He *knew* what she was trying to do, dammit! Was he *teasing* her?

'He's doing very well. Renal function is picking up nicely for the remaining kidney. He'll probably be discharged by the weekend.'

'He's a cute kid.'

'He is.' Paul smiled properly now and once again Jenna couldn't control her response. Smiling back at this man was as natural as breathing. She could feel the knot of tension unravelling inside her. Paul was actually a very *nice* man. Why on earth was she afraid of him?

'I saw you,' she confessed, 'playing with that

toy. Making the animal noises…making Darren laugh.'

The subtle hint of embarrassment in the shrug was charming. Truly arrogant people were never embarrassed, were they?

'Not many surgeons play with their patients,' Jenna continued warmly.

'I love these children,' Paul said simply. 'Their welfare is my life.'

'But…' Jenna hesitated, her heart skipping a beat. No. She *couldn't* say that. Not yet.

'But what?' Paul raised an eyebrow. He leaned a little closer, inviting a response. Demanding one.

'I just wondered…' Jenna gulped in a breath, caution flying to the wind thanks to the warmth in that encouragement. 'You don't…play with Ella much, do you?'

'Scusi?'

That dark gaze was instantly and completely shuttered. Jenna had misjudged the opportunity. Again. But it was too late to back out now.

'Look, I know how much you loved your wife,' Jenna said quietly, 'and I know that being with Ella can't help but remind you of what you've lost, but…' she caught her bottom lip, biting it, forced to look away from the spark of what looked horribly like real anger in Paul's eyes '…she's just a little girl, Paul. A baby. Your *daughter*.'

'And?'

'And…you seem to care more about your patients than you do about *her*.'

'Is that so?' The tone was pure ice. The mug of tea Paul was holding was placed on the bench. With care. Not a drop was spilt despite the amount of fluid still in the vessel. Paul's intake of breath was equally measured. Controlled. 'You are employed as Danielle's nanny,' he said without expression. 'Not as a family counsellor. I suggest you try and remember that.'

To Jenna's utter dismay, she could feel the prickle of tears behind her eyes. She should be feeling angry at this put down but, no, she felt like she'd put her foot in things well and truly.

One step forward.

Three steps back.

Paul's back was very straight. His shoulders square. Jenna was staring at that back now as Paul abandoned his drink and left the kitchen. His words were so quiet she almost didn't hear them, especially as he was facing in the opposite direction.

'What's more,' she thought she heard, 'you're wrong. You have absolutely no idea how wrong you are.'

How dared she?

In his household for all of five minutes and Jenna Freeman thought she'd earned the right to comment on his relationship with Danielle?

To *criticise* him?

Dio!

She was just a woman like every other. She had manipulated him. Pretended attraction and drawn him towards the noose and then used the power his involuntary—and mistaken—steps had granted.

He should fire her.

He *would* fire her.

And then what?

Paul's purposeful stride slowed as he neared the room at the end of the darkened, quiet corridor.

Maria would have to start searching again. She

would try to care for Danielle herself and begin to look as tired and unwell as she had been far too often in the last months.

Maria would never agree to allow Danielle to be taken to Auckland and raised by Louise. And why should she? She adored the baby. The new generation.

Famiglia.

Family.

He couldn't take that away from her.

Paul sighed heavily. He was outside Darren's room now and he couldn't help his sideways glance. The little boy was sound asleep—as he should be—but his mother was awake. Sitting beside the bed with one hand in gentle contact with her son. She looked up and smiled at Paul.

The kind of grateful smile he was accustomed to receiving from his patients' mothers. Paul returned the smile and then his gaze travelled back to the serene face of the sleeping child.

They *were* his life, these children. The unguarded comment that had initiated the criticism from Jenna may have been unwise but it had been perfectly true.

Had her accusations had an element of truth as well?

Would he feel differently about Danielle if she had appeared in his life as one of his patients?

Of course he would. There would have been no need to guard his heart. No reason to employ deliberate avoidance tactics to try and close off a space he had no desire to revisit.

As his anger drained away, something else Jenna had said also rang true.

Danielle was just a little girl. A baby.

None of it was *her* fault.

Not that he needed to feel overly guilty. He was providing all that the child could need. The best of everything money could buy. A nursery fit for royalty. Toys galore. Clothes. The best nanny. And it wasn't that the child wasn't loved. Maria adored her. Louise loved her with an intensity bordering on obsession—a reincarnation of her precious daughter. And now Jenna loved Danielle. Enough to stand up to him and say something she must have known perfectly well he didn't want to hear.

A brave thing to do.

Paul entered Ella's room. His mother had

dozed off in the armchair and the baby was also still asleep. On her back, with her arms flung over her head. Dark lashes lay like butterfly wings above plump cheeks, and rosy lips had a natural curve that was almost a permanent smile.

She was a beautiful child.

For the first time since her birth, Paul looked at Danielle.

Really looked at her.

Taking the perspective of seeing her as a patient instead of his daughter changed everything, really.

She was an *ingenua*. An innocent.

And she was—for better or worse—a part of *his* family.

She deserved more than he had given her thus far in her short life.

Maybe things should change.

Not that he was going to give Jenna the satisfaction of knowing just how much of a nerve she had struck. He was still angry that he had made himself somehow—unintentionally—vulnerable, but he *could* try a little harder, couldn't he?

Make more of an effort to be a father?

For Danielle's sake?

CHAPTER FIVE

HE HATED her.

It took an infinitesimal amount of time—which was all the eye contact afforded when Paul arrived in the nursery the next evening—to know that he was still angry with her.

'How is she?'

The words were clipped and the tone as cool as that brief glance had been.

On the positive side, however, Ella's silky curls got more of a ruffle than the usual flick. She was clearly the focus of attention here.

'Bouncing back.' It was a struggle to sound professional. To ignore the hammering of her heart. Jenna had been dreading this encounter all day, knowing how difficult it would be to see Paul after that little confrontation in the ward kitchen last night. 'Bit of a cough still, but no wheeze or signs of any respiratory distress.'

'Temperature?'

'Been normal since yesterday.' Jenna had Ella perched on one hip as she tidied up after the nappy change. Her charge was eyeing her father with wide and very unsleepy eyes. A damp thumb was removed from her mouth with a popping sound.

'Pa-pa!' Ella announced.

'*Si.*' Paul tilted his head and smiled. 'That's me, *cara.* You are feeling better, yes?'

Good grief! Was Paul actually making an attempt to *converse* with his daughter? Ella seemed as surprised as Jenna. Her hand gripped the arm beneath it more tightly and the spare thumb went back into her mouth. Sucking sounds filled the slightly tense silence.

'You're hungry, aren't you, darling?' Jenna moved towards the microwave that rested on top of a bar fridge in one corner of the spacious nursery. 'Your milk should be ready.'

Surprisingly, Paul seemed in no hurry to go and get his own meal, even though it was 7 p.m. and he'd only just arrived home. He must have left his briefcase and suit jacket by the front door before coming upstairs, and right now he was loosening his tie and undoing the top button of his shirt.

Jenna closed her eyes briefly as she took the warmed bottle from the microwave. She wished she hadn't seen him doing that. It was bound to haunt her in the early hours. Jenna thought the knowledge that she had ruined any chance she might have had to build a more personal relationship with Paul had effectively squashed the desire that she had been all too aware of in the kitchen last night.

Almost effectively, anyway. It had sneaked back some time during the night. Taken on a life of its own, in fact. Amazing how easy it had been to conjure up that awareness…

And how hard to control it. Her mind hadn't stopped with just the memory, had it? Oh, no! Instead of remembering how she'd taken control by offering a cup of tea, Jenna's wakeful brain had invented a journey of its own. One in which she had just waited. Knowing that she would feel the press of his lips against that vulnerable flesh on her neck and his fingers burying themselves in her hair.

One where she turned her head a little and tipped it back to have her throat kissed, and then he cupped her chin and pressed it down so that he could stare at her mouth with the same intensity he had at her neck, and she knew that the next kiss could claim her lips…

Jenna stifled an inward groan. Now she could weave in the sight of those long fingers loosening that tie. Undoing the top button and parting the neck of his shirt.

'She's feeding well?'

Oh, *Lord*! Hadn't Paul left the nursery yet? Jenna pushed the door of the microwave shut, using the loud click as a means of closing off thoughts she shouldn't be encouraging, even in the wakeful, private moments of the night. *Especially* in those moments!

'She's fine.' Paul was standing in front of the chair where Jenna usually sat to give Ella her supper. It could have been an awkward moment but it was saved by Maria bustling into the room.

'Pillows!' she declared. 'And blankets. Paolo! You're home!'

'Yes, Maria.' Paul eyed the armful of bedding his mother was carrying. 'What are you doing?'

'Making a bed for Jenna. She's staying with Ella tonight in case she wakes up.'

'Oh?'

Jenna knew Paul was staring at her. She carefully didn't look back. Was he uncomfortable with the knowledge that his bedroom was beside the nursery? That Jenna would be sleeping just a wall away from him?

'She may be unsettled after her hospital stay,' Jenna said calmly. 'It's just for a night or two.'

Ella gave a small whimper and reached for her bottle. Jenna had to move.

'Excuse me,' she murmured as she brushed past Paul. 'I need to sit down to feed Ella.'

'Of course. Sorry.' But Paul seemed slightly bemused and stepped in the same direction as Jenna. His body bumped her arm. If the effect of seeing him unbutton his shirt collar was going to be in her memory bank for involuntary perusal, the reminder of what actual physical contact was like would be an equally hefty deposit.

This was getting ridiculous.

He hates you, Jenna reminded herself. You told him he sucked at being a dad. That he had a better relationship with his patients than his daughter. And to top it off, you reminded him how much he had loved his wife.

If she'd wanted to write a manual on how to kill even the possibility of a man fancying you, she couldn't have opened with a better ploy.

Not that she wanted a relationship. Or not an intimate one. Jenna had to refocus on her original goal and it was a good thing that they had stepped away from the minefield of physical attraction that had just appeared from nowhere to surround them. The sooner she put all thoughts of Paul as a man out of her head the better.

She'd think of him as Dr Romano, Jenna decided. Famous surgeon. Or, better yet, just as Ella's father.

That was good. No chance of forgetting her mission that way.

It became easier to think of Paul simply as Ella's father because he seemed to be embarked on a campaign to spend more time with his daughter. Had something of what she'd said sunk in?

If so, it was worth the personal sacrifice of driving Paul away from the distracting possibility of exploring that chemical attraction. Jenna could find satisfaction in being a martyr to a higher cause.

She could also be pleased with having the presence of mind to get dressed *and* brush her hair the moment she heard movements in the adjacent room that morning, because Paul poked his head around the door before he even went downstairs for breakfast.

'She's still asleep, then?' Was he relieved or disappointed? The tone was too neutral to analyse.

'She had an unsettled night.'

'Yes. I heard her crying.'

Had Paul been as aware of her through the wall as she had been of him? 'I hope it didn't disturb you too much.'

'I'm quite used to being disturbed at night.' But Paul was looking uncomfortable now. He cleared his throat. 'It's good that you stayed with her. My mother is getting too old to be up and down all night to Danielle.'

Not that Jenna would dare say it aloud but the thought that Paul might consider getting up to comfort his daughter himself couldn't be repressed. And maybe it showed on her face because, when Jenna risked the tiniest glance, she was met by a distinctly stony stare.

But something *had* changed.

Despite most probably hating her, Paul was still drawn back to the nursery as soon as he returned home that evening. He looked very tired.

'Maria said to say goodnight. She's off at her cooking class.'

Jenna nodded her acknowledgement. She was busy changing Ella's nappy. Chubby legs kicked up at her from the padded table and it was impossible to fasten the sticky tapes so Jenna caught both feet with one hand.

'You're full of beans tonight, aren't you, chicken? There. All done.' Jenna stuck the second tab down. Without thinking, she did what she always did on completing this particular task, ducking her head to blow a raspberry on Ella's bare tummy.

The baby shrieked with delight—a sound that subsided into her delicious, drainpipe gurgle, and it wasn't until Jenna turned to pick up the clean sleepsuit that she realised what Paul had just witnessed.

He didn't look angry, though. If anything, he had that faintly bemused air she had noticed when Maria had been moving her into the nursery for the night. As though he was in unfamiliar territory and unsure of the protocol. A woman's domain, perhaps, which could explain why he had made no protest at the idea of Jenna sleeping next door.

Then, as Ella's giggle continued, Paul smiled.

A smile that started slowly with crinkles at the corners of his eyes just before his lips moved. An unconscious response to the joyful noise Ella was creating. And then it grew until it stretched into a grin.

Jenna smiled, too.

And the tension that had been between them ever since that exchange in the ward kitchen suddenly evaporated.

'She's a happy little thing, isn't she?' Paul sounded as though this was a new discovery.

'She's gorgeous,' Jenna responded firmly. 'She's the most wonderful baby in the world. Aren't you?' She tickled Ella just to make her laugh again and then got on with the serious business of stuffing those fat little arms and legs into the soft, terry-towelling suit.

'I'll have to put you down for a minute,' she warned Ella, 'while I make up your milk.' She wasn't about to risk destroying this new ambience by suggesting that Paul hold his daughter.

When she put Ella down on the carpet, the baby went into a fast crawl, making a beeline for her father. Reaching shiny, black shoes, Ella crowed with delight and tugged at the laces. Then she grabbed a fistful of pinstripe trousers.

Jenna watched from the corner of her eye as she spooned formula into the bottle and added distilled water. Sure enough, Ella wriggled her little bottom, planted her feet and used her grip on the trousers to lever herself up.

'Hey!' Paul was watching, dumbfounded.

'It's her new trick,' Jenna said proudly. 'She did

it for the first time this afternoon. I'll bet she'll be walking in no time.'

Poor Paul. He clearly didn't know what to do. Ella was attached to his trousers like a large leech and beaming triumphantly up at him but swaying precariously. Any movement from her anchor and she would topple.

Which she did, anyway, just as Jenna pushed the start button on the microwave to heat the milk.

'Oops!' She swooped to pick Ella up before a second attempt could be made, but Paul had backed away.

'I'd better go and find my dinner,' he said uncomfortably.

'Sure.' Jenna settled Ella on her hip and pointed to the microwave. 'How many seconds, Ella? See? Ten...nine...eight...'

'Um...' Paul had paused by the door. 'Have you eaten, Jenna?'

'No. I'll get Ella settled first.'

'I'll save some of Maria's lasagne for you, then.'

The offer was startling but maybe it was a kind of peace offering. To underline the exit of that tension. It would be rude to say that she had been planning some instant noodles in front of television in her flat. So Jenna smiled.

'That would be great, thank you.'

Why had he said that?

And why on earth was he still pottering around the kitchen three quarters of an hour later, filling a basket with slices of a crusty French bread stick and debating which of the two very good red wines he had pulled from the cellar was the one he should open?

Anyone would think this was some kind of a *date*.

He just wanted a chance to talk to Jenna, that was all. Not that he was intending to apologise for a second time, but he wanted Jenna to know that he wasn't the monster she clearly thought he was. He wanted to ask questions. To show an interest in Danielle.

And maybe he also wanted someone to talk to at the end of a long and difficult day.

Someone who might understand.

* * *

'They're not very common, are they? Choledochal cysts?' Jenna finally appeared to have recovered from her astonishment at finding a place set for her at a kitchen table laden with bread, salad, wine and a deep dish of lasagne that gave off the most mouth watering aroma of meat and cheese.

'No. Only about one in one hundred thousand live births in Western Europe.' Paul was watching Jenna's hands as she took a round slice of bread and then tore it into two pieces. She had astonishingly beautiful hands. Delicate but strong at the same time. He had seen those hands busy snapping drug ampoules, finding a difficult vein and then slipping in a needle. Clever hands. Competent.

Suddenly realising he had been staring a little too long, Paul cleared his throat. 'They're a lot more common in Japan. They get one in a thousand.'

'And it's more common in females, isn't it?'

'Yes. A ratio of one to four.'

'The opposite of hypertrophic pyloric stenosis, then.'

'Exactly opposite.' The pleasant surprise was the same as he'd feel if one of his students had

shown themselves to be unexpectedly knowl-
edgeable. Wasn't it? 'That's four to one in favour
of males. Far more common, too. About three per
one thousand births.'

'So it was a difficult operation for the cyst?'

'This kid was pretty sick. The cyst wasn't diagnosed early enough and she presented with
billary fibrosis, cirrhosis and liver failure.'

'She presented with abdo pain, I guess? And
jaundice?'

'And vomiting. She'd been complaining of tum-
myaches off and on for the last eighteen months.
The GP had diagnosed childhood migraine.'

Jenna's eyebrows had risen. It made her eyes
wider than usual. Those little gold flecks more
obvious. 'She's not a neonate, then?'

Paul blinked, deliberately shutting off the fascination of the gold flecks. 'No. She's nearly six.
Would you believe a phobia of starting school
was offered as the initial diagnosis?'

'Family problems?'

'Yes. Big family. Big, poor family.'

'Poor wee thing.'

Why was he surprised that Jenna could see

straight to the heart of the matter? She must have been a damned good nurse. Bit of a waste to have her shut away caring for a single, healthy baby.

'Has it made a lot of difference to her prognosis? The delay?'

'Hell, yes! Possibly the difference between regression of the liver fibrosis and return of normal hepatic function and needing a liver transplant.'

'Oh…' Jenna's sigh captured everything Paul had been feeling about the case. 'How did the surgery go?'

'I wasn't happy. Only the mucosa of the cyst was removable with jejunal anastomosis to the proximal bile duct. Better than nothing but with the evidence of atresia…' Paul echoed Jenna's sigh. Then he made a deliberate effort to smile. 'Enough shop talk, anyway. Hardly what you want over dinner.'

'Actually…' Jenna smiled back '…it's exactly what I like over dinner. I miss it.'

'The nursing?' He had been right. Jenna was wasted in this position as a nanny and she knew it. Funny how the thought of her going back to where she belonged created such a sinking feeling in his gut.

'Medicine in general,' Jenna nodded. 'It's my world. Always had been. My father was a doctor, my mother was a nurse. That's how they met, of course.'

'Of course.' But Paul didn't want to go there.

'Dad died six years ago with an MI and Mum…I think she gave up on life after Dad died. I never got the feeling she fought too hard against the cancer.'

'So you're an orphan? Poor you!'

Jenna shook her head. Just enough to make the soft curls bounce against her shoulders. 'Being an orphan suggests dependency, doesn't it? Thirty-one is getting a bit old to expect sympathy for losing both parents.'

'Sympathy is always called for given the loss of family. I will never forget the trauma of losing my father and I'm nowhere near ready to contemplate not having my mother around.'

Dio, but Jenna's eyes looked huge at the moment. Shining with something that looked curiously like gratitude, mixed with unshed tears, perhaps. It made him feel as though he had given her something precious rather than simply an understanding of what she'd been through. It made him feel benevolent. Generous. Powerful, even.

The sensation was pleasant enough to make him want to give her more.

A lot more.

With an effort, Paul dragged his gaze away yet again.

'Eat,' he commanded. ' Maria will be offended if there are leftovers.'

Jenna ate.

Fast enough to risk indigestion.

Why had Paul done this? Set a table and then waited so that he could share his meal with her? It made her feel like he'd wanted her company.

That he didn't hate her after all.

The roadblock to the path she knew she shouldn't even contemplate stepping onto had been unexpectedly removed. And the temptation was wicked!

Jenna could only think of one way to avoid succumbing to that temptation and that was to remove herself from Paul's company as quickly as possible. So she ate fast and answered his questions as succinctly as she could between bites without appearing rude.

Yes, she loved nursing—especially children.

No, she had never wanted to be a doctor like her father. She liked the more personal involvement with her patients that nursing afforded.

Yes, she was enjoying Christchurch. She could see why it was called 'The Garden City'.

Yes, Ella seemed almost fully recovered now. Happy, despite some new teeth that were starting to emerge.

No, she didn't need any new toys or equipment to help her learn to walk. She would get there quite fast enough on her own.

And, no, she couldn't possibly eat another mouthful of food.

Or sit there a moment longer when every minute of listening to the sound of Paul's voice or seeing him tear a piece of bread or fork food into his mouth threatened to undermine any resolve she had made to think of him purely as Ella's father.

It was becoming way too difficult.

* * *

It became even harder over the course of the weekend.

Paul had done a ward round in the morning but he was at home for lunch and the day was so nice Maria had deemed they should have the meal outside in the cobbled courtyard beneath a pergola that was densely covered by a mature grapevine. Ella and Jenna had been included in the leisurely feast of bread and cheese and ham with all sorts of olives and other morsels of finger food.

'You should go, Jenna,' Maria said finally. 'This is your afternoon off.'

'I'll wait until Ella goes down for her nap.' Jenna caught Maria's gaze. She wanted to check Maria's blood-glucose level before she left the house for the shopping trip and then the dinner she had arranged to have with Anne. Having established control more easily than expected, Dr Barry was allowing Maria to try only two insulin injections a day, but the glucose levels still needed frequent evaluation.

'She doesn't look very sleepy,' Paul observed

from over the rim of his glass of red wine. 'In spite of all that bread she's stuffed into herself.'

'No.' Jenna lifted Ella from the high chair. 'I'll let her crawl on the grass for a bit. She loves being outside.'

But Ella wasn't content to crawl. She wanted to stand.

It was unfortunate that Louise chose to let herself into the Romano household unannounced and then go to find the family outside in the garden. The distraction she produced was enough for attention to be off Ella for just a second or two.

Long enough for small hands to grasp the edge of the tablecloth hanging at just the right height. An anchor that probably looked as secure as Paul's trousers had but which proved thoroughly unreliable as Ella pulled on it to heave herself upright.

The crash of the first plate onto the cobblestones was more than enough to alert them all to impending disaster. Ella's small, trusting face was turned upwards, oblivious to the heavy platter of cold meats now sliding rapidly towards the edge of the table.

'*Dio!*' Paul moved so swiftly he was blur in Jenna's peripheral vision. He snatched Ella up and away as several more items crashed around her.

Startled, and then frustrated, Ella let out a bellow, but Paul simply lifted her higher.

'Flying baby,' he pronounced, proceeding to swoop Ella in a huge arc.

Her threatened wail of distress turned into a surprised squeak as she reached the top of the arc and then became a cry of delight as she fell backwards, cocooned in the safety of two large, strong hands cradling her body. Paul then swung her in a circle around him and she started laughing.

The three women stood among the shards of china and spilt food on the cobblestones, oblivious to the destruction around their feet.

Or even the near miss of Ella badly injuring herself.

And then Jenna began to smile.

Paul was *playing* with his daughter.

She looked at Maria and wasn't surprised to see the older woman catching a tear as it escaped her eye.

When she heard the sound of Paul actually

laughing aloud for the first time, Jenna felt the prickle of tears of her own.

Paul was not only playing with Ella.

He was *loving* it.

He stopped whirling the baby before she could become giddy and then, there he was, with Ella in his arms, standing still and staring at Jenna, who was grinning like an idiot.

Paul was also grinning and the connection it created between them was so powerful Jenna felt like she standing on the edge of a precipice.

About to fall.

And she was.

At that moment Jenna was in terrible danger of falling…in love.

With a man who was not only stunningly attractive but perfectly capable of loving his own child.

He did already. Like Maria had said, maybe he just hadn't realised it.

But why not?

The answer came as Paul's grin faded and his gaze slid sideways.

'Oh. My. God,' Louise said with deliberate emphasis. 'What in heaven's name is going on?'

Jenna stepped towards Paul. She needed to hold Ella. To justify her presence in this group. To have an excuse to escape before Louise's gimlet gaze could detect body language that might reflect thoughts that even Jenna wasn't ready to deal with.

Paul seemed more than happy to relinquish Ella. He seemed to have collected himself and had that vaguely bewildered air again. Perhaps he was as astounded at his own behaviour as everyone else had been.

'Thanks, Jenna,' he said crisply. 'I'll find a broom and clear this mess up.'

'But what happened?' Louise demanded.

'Ella has learned to stand up in the last couple of days,' Jenna said. 'Trouble is, she needs something to hang onto and doesn't know about tablecloths.'

'You weren't *watching* her?' Louise was outraged. 'She could have been badly hurt! What if one of those dishes had landed on—?'

'It's not Jenna's fault,' Paul interrupted smoothly. 'We were all here with Ella.'

'Yes.' The word carried a wealth of innuendo. Too much. Jenna could feel herself flushing. It had been a family scene. A picnic lunch in the garden. Why *had* Maria insisted she join them? And thank God Louise hadn't seen her having dinner with Paul last night.

'I must go,' she said aloud. It was time to ease the tension by reminding everyone of her status as an employee. Including herself. 'It *is* my afternoon off after all.'

'I'll come in, too,' Maria said hastily. 'To find the broom.'

'I'll take Danielle, then, shall I?' Louise made it sound as though she had arrived in the nick of time. 'Perhaps you could find me a coffee-cup while you're inside, Maria.'

The spell away from the Romano family was well timed. It gave Jenna breathing space and, in time-honoured fashion, a chance to determine how she was feeling by having an intimate discussion with a close female friend.

'I should probably resign right now. Maybe I'm not needed. Paul is starting to act like a *real* father.'

'Since when?' Anne countered. She didn't wait for a response from Jenna. 'Since you told him he cared more about his patients than his own child, that's when. This is your doing, Jenna, and it's only just begun. Disappear now and I guarantee things will revert to exactly how they were before you arrived.'

'But how can I stay? It's impossible!'

'Why, because you think you might be love with Paul? Why don't you stay long enough to find out how he feels about you?' Anne's grin was wicked. 'You might succeed where many have tried and failed.'

'No.' Jenna's head shake was virtually a shudder. 'You should have seen the way Louise was looking at me. I'd be dead meat if she knew. I might be already because I'm sure she's suspicious.'

'Nothing's happened,' Anne soothed. 'And nothing will…unless you want it to.'

'I *don't*!'

'Really?'

'Yes…no…oh, I don't know, Anne. I'm confused.'

'I'm thinking that Paul probably is as well. What *was* with that romantic dinner the other night?'

'I have no idea.'

'You do want him to bond with Ella, though, don't you?'

'Of course.'

'So see it through. Make sure that bond is as strong as it can be. Then you can decide what you want to do about Doctor Romantico.'

CHAPTER SIX

As IF the decision was ever going to be hers!

Jenna realised just how wrong Anne had been in making that assumption at precisely 3 a.m. the next morning.

She hadn't heard a telephone ring but maybe that was what had woken Ella. By the time Jenna had stumbled over to the cot the baby was asleep again. Jenna was still half-asleep herself, otherwise she might have thought to grab a robe before heading out of the nursery towards the bathroom.

She woke up fast enough on the return journey when a dark figure seemed to materialise in front of her. Paul was fully dressed. Not in a suit, of course, but the faded jeans and black jersey were perfectly respectable.

Unlike Jenna's silk boxer shorts or the singlet top with a scrap of lace at the bottom of its deep

V neck and a hemline that failed to cover her belly button thanks to how much it had shrunk in the wash.

Instinctively, she stepped aside, although the upstairs hallway was more than wide enough for a whole group of people to pass. She put a hand out to touch the wall as though hoping, by some magic, it would pull her in and make her invisible.

It felt, horribly, as though she was standing stark naked in front of Paul Romero.

'I…um…had to use the bathroom,' she faltered.

'Are you unwell?'

'No!' Was that why he was staring at her with an intensity even the dimmest light couldn't disguise? Physical awareness hummed between them and it took an incredible effort of will for Jenna to break that eye contact. 'Not at all. I only woke because Ella did. She's fine. She's asleep again.'

She was babbling. Too uncomfortable to do anything but look desperately past Paul, hunting for an escape route. He was a large man, certainly, but he wasn't exactly blocking her way. Why wouldn't her feet obey the simple command to move?

'I imagine the phone woke her. I have to go in to the hospital. That little girl I told you about seems to be running into trouble. Liver failure.'

'Oh…I'm sorry. I'd better not hold you up.'

'No. Sleep well, Jenna.'

As if! But it wasn't as if Paul had been staring at her body. The intense gaze Jenna had been sucked into before managing to avert her eyes so determinedly had been directed at her face.

So why did her body feel…scorched? Why was she still tossing and turning and awake enough to hear Paul's return two hours later? Jenna had to give up any possibility of sleep at that point as she imagined him peeling off those jeans and climbing wearily into his own bed to snatch another hour or two of rest if he was lucky.

It was high time she moved back into the flat. Ella didn't need her nanny sharing the nursery any longer and Jenna *had* to create some distance for her own peace of mind.

A week later, Jenna was congratulating herself on how well the strategy was working.

Louise didn't appear to be suspicious any

longer. She had stopped watching Jenna's every move and trying to analyse her facial expressions if Paul was at home. She seemed, instead, to be sharing Maria's fascination with the way he was interacting with Ella.

And interacting he was. Virtually every day. He played with his daughter. One day he sprawled, still in his pinstripe suit, on the lounge floor within minutes of arriving home.

He built towers of bright plastic cups, discussing the colours as though they were as intellectually stimulating as a peer-reviewed article in one of his surgical journals.

'This one is *giallo*. Yellow. A very bright yellow. You get sunflowers this colour and maybe a very ripe lemon.' The yellow cup was balanced carefully on top of the blue one. 'And this one is *rosso*. Red. *Scarlotto*. If it was darker, it would be *color cremisi*. Crimson. It's smaller than the yellow cup, see? It fits on top. And right up here we're going to put the little pink one. What happens now, Ella?'

Ella knew. Her face changed from the dreamy contentment of listening to the deep rumble of her father's voice and her eyes crinkled in pure mischief just a fraction of a second before her lips curled into a wide smile.

Just the way her father's did.

Ella raised her hand, leaned forward and shoved hard enough to topple the rainbow tower.

'Yes! Shall we build it again, *cara*?'

Ella clapped her hands—another new skill— and Maria sighed happily and then sniffed and reached for a tissue. Louise, present on that occasion, simply watched with a carefully benign smile.

Neither of the grandmothers were present on the Thursday of the following week, a day when Paul often managed to get home a little earlier after one of his clinics.

Jenna was sitting, cross-legged, on the floor, thinking it was time to start tidying up the scattered toys.

Paul was bent over so far he had to be hurting his back. Ella had been standing beside a couch as he'd entered the lounge and he had responded to the commanding little hand that waved at him.

Now he was holding both Ella's hands as she stood in front of him, beaming and swaying.

And then it happened. Instead of the usual plonk onto her well-padded bottom, Ella lifted a bare foot and lurched forward. Paul instinctively adjusted the space between them and it happened again. The other tiny foot lifted and stepped forward. And Ella was still on her feet, grinning up at her father.

But he was looking at Jenna.

'Did you see that, Jenna? Did you see it?' His face shone with pride and the words tumbled out excitedly. 'She took her first step! Her *first* step!'

'Yes.' The pride was contagious. A spark ignited somewhere deep and Jenna could feel the glow radiating through her body.

'It was the first, wasn't it?' An anxious frown creased Paul's forehead. 'She hasn't been doing this when I'm not around, has she?'

'No.' Jenna had to smile but there was a poignancy in the mix of emotions as she watched Paul lift Ella for a congratulatory cuddle.

She loved the pride she saw. The satisfaction in having been there to witness a new milestone. The relief in knowing that the bond between father and daughter was growing stronger every day.

But most of all she loved it that they were sharing this moment. Like…

Like any proud parents.

She was too involved.

Travelling too far down a path that could only lead to heartbreak.

It didn't help that Maria was determined to make her a part of the family. Like when she insisted that Jenna join them to celebrate her birthday a couple of weeks later.

'But you must come, *cara*. You and Ella. I am making my special risotto. It is a *celebrazione*. For *famiglia*. It could not be complete without you, Jenna.'

And Jenna agreed readily because she loved Maria. Loved feeling like part of this small family. Mothered, even. Every day, Maria would ask how well she had slept. Would comment if she thought Jenna looked tired or pale and asked, so often, if she was happy. She would insist that Jenna taste any recipe she was practising for her cooking classes and frequently made special treats for a meal or snack just because she wanted to. Jenna felt as cared for and petted as Ella sometimes and she couldn't deny that it was healing the very raw patch on her soul that her own mother's death had left.

It wasn't a one-way street by any means. Jenna was proud of the way Paul's mother was getting both braver and more competent with the management of her diabetes. Maria could measure her own blood-glucose level now but she still depended on Jenna to administer the insulin injections.

And she still refused to let Paul know about the change in her medical condition. Jenna had tried hard to persuade her. Increasingly, she didn't like Paul not knowing. It was like lying by omission. A wedge that separated her from being a real part of the family.

'He has to know,' she had said more than once. 'It's important, Maria. You should be wearing a medic-alert bracelet and someone other than myself and Shirley and Dr Barry needs to know.'

'Why?'

'Just in case something goes wrong. Not that it's likely to,' she added reassuringly as a fearful expression appeared on Maria's face. 'It's just…important.'

'Not yet,' Maria had said decisively. 'Not until I can manage—all by myself. I do not want Paolo to think I am *vigliacca*…a… What is the word for someone who is silly by being scared?'

Jenna had grinned. 'A wimp?'

'*Si*. I do not want to be a wimp.'

But Jenna knew there was more to it than that and it worried her, becoming another aspect to why the thought of leaving to return to her nursing position was becoming harder every day.

Yes, she felt like part of the family, but she also felt distanced. Was that how Louise felt? Jenna still didn't understand some of the bonds but they were there and strengthening. A strength that became suddenly a lot more obvious on a day the following week.

A Wednesday, when Louise was there. She arrived, as usual, before breakfast was complete and while she had coffee, they were planning

Ella's first birthday party, which was only a few weeks away.

Or rather, Louise was planning it. Maria wanted just a family occasion. Louise was determined to have the house filled with balloons and flowers. To hire a magician and possibly a pony as well.

'She's a baby, Louise,' Maria protested. 'She won't remember. All she needs is love.'

'She'll see the photographs when she's older.' Louise had made a note. 'I must book a photographer. Danielle will look back in years to come and she will know how much her grandmother loved her.'

Maria scowled. Louise glared. Ella was oblivious to the tension, however, and banged her spoon on her plate.

'Nen -nah!' she declared.

Louise gasped. 'She said *Nana*! She knows who I am!'

Maria shook her head. 'I think it was *Nonna*. Paul is teaching her Italian. *Nonna* is Italian for grandmother.'

Jenna said nothing, so close to tears it wasn't funny. Paul had certainly taught Ella the new word but it was as close as the little girl had been able to get…to *Jenna*.

The bonds were tightening.

It was going to be very hard for Jenna to leave the Romano household.

But not impossible.

The idea that it could, in fact, become unbearable was born just a day later. On Thursday, when Paul had been held up after his clinic by a departmental meeting and didn't arrive home until 6.30 p.m.

When Ella was having her bath.

He'd never ventured into the bathroom to include himself in this part of the daily routine so it was something to be celebrated that he only seemed a little hesitant to do so. Jenna's smile of welcome was sincerely delighted but she felt obliged to issue a warning.

'You might not want to get that suit wet. Ella can get a bit excited in the bath.' Too late now to worry about how wet her own clothing might be. Whether her T-shirt was clinging a little too closely in places that might not be appropriate.

'It's only a suit.' Paul smiled back. That delicious, *real* smile, so like his daughter's, where the corners of his eyes crinkled just before his lips curved. He sat on the closed lid of the toilet, watching as Jenna rinsed shampoo from Ella's dark curls, which were almost long enough to hold a ribbon now.

Ella played with a flotilla of plastic ducks, once clutched firmly in each hand as she stirred the shampoo suds collecting on the surface of the water. Jenna concentrated on soaping her charge's chubby body, which wasn't easy because Ella wriggled and giggled and waved the ducks in the air. The task usually kept a smile on Jenna's face all on its own. That Paul was also there should have made the time far more joyous but Jenna couldn't help the poignancy that stole through her.

The bond between father and daughter was so much stronger now. It would still be there when Jenna was gone.

She should be happy that she was succeeding in her mission. Ridiculous to feel bereft imagining total success. That she wouldn't be needed any longer. Wouldn't be missed…

Ella smacked her ducks onto the water hard enough to splash soapy water onto both Jenna and Paul. He didn't seem to mind. He wasn't even annoyed when Ella threw a duck at him. Laughing, he slid down to kneel on the bathmat beside Jenna to return the toy. Close enough to touch his daughter's cheek.

Close enough for his hip to be touching Jenna's. For her to feel the warmth of his whole body. The warmth of her *own* body, which seemed to be increasing at an alarming rate.

Ella thanked her father by scooping up handfuls of bubbles. Her offering was enthusiastic enough to leave her hands at speed. Her aim was off, however, and the soapy suds missed him and landed on Jenna's face. She shook her head, laughing, but then glanced up at Paul to see if he was sharing her amusement.

And that was a huge mistake.

He wasn't laughing. He wasn't even smiling, and the look Jenna was receiving seemed to turn her to stone.

No, not stone.

A stone could never feel this…*alive*.

She was just still. Waiting. Because time had stopped.

Like that moment in the ward kitchen. Or the one in the upstairs hallway. Only this time Paul wasn't going to distract himself by attending to his duty. And Jenna was not going to distract either of them by offering a cup of tea. Or attending to her own duty other than keeping hold of a slippery baby. She couldn't do anything else.

Jenna was incapable of doing anything other than waiting.

Even Ella seemed to be waiting. Jenna could feel the baby's stillness, although she couldn't see it because her gaze was locked on Paul's. The incomprehensible babble of contented sounds from the bath had also ceased. Or maybe Jenna just couldn't hear them any more because her awareness was so totally focussed on the man beside her.

As his was. On her.

He lifted his hand, using his middle finger to smooth a blob of soap suds from just below her eye. The touch was so light, so intense, it could be nothing less than a caress.

Then he stroked another away from her cheek. Only this time his finger didn't leave her skin. It traced a line from her cheek to the corner of her mouth and Jenna's lips parted involuntarily as the finger kept moving.

It wasn't a conscious decision to touch the tip of that finger with her tongue. She would have done it instinctively to catch the taste of him on her lips and it was simply that Paul's movements were so slow and deliberate that she hadn't been able to wait.

The connection unleashed something almost frightening. Jenna wouldn't have believed that Paul's eyes could darken that much. Or that she would ever hear him utter a sound that was pure, raw desire.

'You,' he said very softly, 'are beautiful. *Bella.*'

And then, with Jenna completely helpless as she held Ella safely upright in her bath, Paul tipped his head and kissed her.

Softly.

Slowly.

With the same deliberate touch his finger had made.

It wasn't enough. Not nearly enough, and Jenna knew Paul was thinking exactly the same because her gaze was still locked onto his—as it had been from the first moment he had touched her face.

There was no question of whether or not they would make love. It was simply a matter of when.

Which was most definitely not going to be now!

'I…I need to dry Ella and get her to bed.' Jenna almost groaned aloud. How stupid was that, to utter the word 'bed' when sexual tension heavy enough to be practically flattening them both had not even begun to dissipate?

The quirk of Paul's eyebrow revealed absolute comprehension. The lopsided curve to his mouth suggested both resignation and amusement.

'Of course you do. And I need to help Maria in the kitchen. Louise is coming to dinner tonight.' The flash of distaste in his expression eased a significant part of the tension. 'Apparently she wishes her new boyfriend to meet her granddaughter.'

Jenna nodded, lifting Ella from the bath and ignoring her squeak of protest as she wrapped her in a soft, fluffy towel. 'Yes. I'm to bring her down for a few minutes before her bedtime.'

'You'll come back, won't you? When Ella is asleep?'

Jenna stared. Did Paul realise that this was the first time he had ever used the diminutive of his daughter's name?

He misunderstood her hesitation.

'Please, come,' he said softly. 'As Maria said on her birthday, you are one of the family now.'

His gaze dropped to her mouth and Jenna watched, mesmerised, as he slowly licked his lips.

'You belong,' he added simply, 'with *me*.'

CHAPTER SEVEN

'SHE'S a princess, Lulu. An absolute princess!'

Ella was sitting on Gerald Bagshaw's lap. A rather slippery lap because the pants were a very tight fit, but Ella didn't seem to mind. She was staring with open-mouthed fascination at the heavy gold chain resting on a thick patch of dark hair the open-necked shirt was revealing. Jenna watched with some concern as small pink fingers started their journey towards the chain but her lips twitched.

Lulu?

The cough that came from Paul's direction could well have been a disguised snort of amusement. Jenna risked a quick glance as Maria screened Louise by offering an antipasto platter laden with pâté spread on crostini, pickles and cold meats.

Sure enough, there was a look of unholy glee in his dark eyes that had to be because of learning the pet name Gerald had for Louise.

'Try one of these stuffed olives, Jenna. My own recipe. You'll love them.'

Jenna thanked Maria and chose one of the fat green olives, but it wasn't enough of a distraction. Surely the tension generated by that kiss should have evaporated by now—nearly an hour after Ella's bathtime? But it hadn't. She had discovered that the moment she set'd foot in the formal lounge.

There it was all over again.

That kiss.

Just hanging in the air between them, like a ticking clock.

Or maybe an unexploded bomb.

Nervously, Jenna flicked another glance in Paul's direction at the precise moment she was opening her mouth to eat her olive. No hint of amusement on Paul's face now. He actually closed his eyes as he shifted uncomfortably on the overstuffed wing chair. Jenna knew exactly what he was thinking. She was thinking the same thing the instant the tip of her tongue touched the olive.

Oh, *help*! This was going to be a lot harder than she had anticipated.

Jenna would have to find an excuse not to join the Romano family for dinner. At least they weren't planning to eat in the kitchen as they usually did, but the formal dining room wasn't that far away. And the kitchen was only a few steps away from Jenna's apartment. Who would know if Paul chose to visit her there late at night?

Tonight, even?

The olive was proving difficult to swallow, until Jenna's glance slid sideways to find Louise staring at her. Then it went down painfully fast. How long had she been watching? Had she seen the way Paul had almost visibly winced as he'd watched her putting the olive in her mouth?

Gerald let out a timely squeak as a small fist tugged on his chest hair.

'Lu?'

Louise had to move to rescue Gerald. She tried to prise Ella's fingers clear. 'It's your chain she likes, Gerry. She's not really trying to torture you.'

'She's a princess,' Gerald repeated with a sigh

of relief as Louise lifted Ella from his lap. 'Good taste 'n' all. Twenty-four-carat gold this chain is. Cost a bomb! I bought it to celebrate my first million, y'know.'

'What is it that you do, Gerald?' Paul's question was courteous.

'Septic tanks,' Gerald told him proudly. 'There's a lot of money in sh—'

'Gerry!' Louise's reprimand was coquettish.

'Sorry, pumpkin.' Gerald licked his lips as he watched Louise walk back to her chair, getting a rear view of the way her black dress clung to slim hips. 'Hard to believe she's a grandmother, eh? I said I *wouldn't* believe it. Show me the evidence, I said.'

The evidence was now scowling at him over Louise's shoulder. Jenna could feel Paul's gaze but refused to look in his direction. She couldn't lighten the atmosphere by shared amusement at how awful this visitor was. Did Louise really see him as a potential life partner? Was it just the blatant show of available spending power or did he have hidden qualities like…like being a totally amazing lover?

As Jenna knew with absolute certainty Paul was going to be. She mimicked his earlier gesture, closing her eyes for a second to try and regain control. It seemed to help. She was able to focus on someone other than Paul when she opened them again.

Maybe Gerald wouldn't appear so brash in another setting, she decided. Like a beach barbecue, perhaps. It could be that the discreet and tasteful wealth of the Romano family was highlighting a very different set of values. Whatever the reason, nobody was feeling comfortable.

'Would you like to try an olive, Gerald?' Maria, typically, was trying to fix whatever was wrong by offering food. 'Or some prosciutto?'

'Proshy what?'

'Ham,' Paul supplied.

Gerald eyed the platter with deep suspicion. 'I'm a steak and potatoes man myself,' he declared. 'Always have been. Still, it'd be rude not to, eh?' He fumbled for an olive. 'Might need a drop more bourbon to wash it down with, mind.'

'Allow me.' Paul's lips seemed thinner than

usual as he moved to refill Gerald's glass but Jenna couldn't tell whether he was trying to suppress amusement or understandable irritation.

Ella's lips were also compressed but her expression was far easier to interpret. She had twisted in Louise's arms to try and catch sight of the glittering treasure around Gerald's neck. The prize she had been denied.

'It's getting past Ella's bedtime,' Jenna said hurriedly in an attempt to avoid disaster. 'Should I take her upstairs?'

'You're the nanny, right?' Gerald stopped watching the rising level of spirits in his glass to leer at Jenna. Then he frowned at Paul before returning his gaze to Jenna. 'You a relative?'

'No!' Jenna was horrified. Was the electricity between herself and Paul detectable even to a complete stranger?

'You just look kinda Italian,' Gerald pronounced. He took another long appreciative look as he nodded.

Louise's eyes narrowed. 'I think it would be a very good idea if you took Danielle upstairs now, Jennifer.'

Jenna rose swiftly, but not before Ella opened

her mouth to let everyone know just how tired and frustrated she was. Louise raised her voice over the bellow but still managed to sound casual.

'While you're in the nursery, Jennifer, could you keep an eye out for my gold watch? I'm wondering if I might have left it beside the change table somewhere.'

'Oh?' Jenna couldn't remember when Louise had last offered to change a nappy. Or set foot in the nursery even. She usually waited downstairs, sipping her black coffee, while Jenna got Ella ready for her outings.

Gerald's glass paused in mid-air. 'Not the watch *I* gave you, was it, pumpkin?'

Louise favoured him with a very apologetic look. 'I'm afraid so, Gerry. Ella took a fancy to playing with it, just like she did with your chain.'

'Good taste.' Gerald nodded. 'Told you so.'

'I took it off,' Louise continued smoothly, 'because I didn't want it to get dirty.'

'Or broken!' Gerald eyed the now howling Ella and nodded approvingly. 'She's got a grip like a gorilla, the little monkey!'

* * *

The 'little monkey' rubbed her nose on Jenna's shoulder and hiccuped sadly. Jenna kissed her and made for the door, noticing a rather odd expression on Paul's face as she paused to let him say good-night to his daughter. He stood up and leaned close.

'I'll come up, too, shall I?' he murmured, quietly enough not to be overheard. 'And help tuck Ella in?'

Jenna's eyes widened in alarm. That would really set Louise off. Then she caught the ghost of a wink from Paul.

'Take no notice,' he said. Then he kissed Ella gently on each cheek, ruffled her hair and raised his voice. *'Buona notte, cara. A presto domani.'*

It did weird things to Jenna's knees when she heard Paul speak in Italian but luckily it didn't show as she walked through the door he was now holding open for her.

Maria followed. 'I must check on dinner,' she excused herself.

Jenna waited until the door closed behind them. 'Are you feeling all right, Maria? Have you checked your blood sugar?'

'I'm fine.'

'Are you sure? You look a little pale.'

'I am *arrabbiata*. Angry! It starts all over again!'

Jenna rocked Ella who was almost asleep in her arms. She would be able to take her upstairs and simply slip her into bed in a minute. She should do it right now but there was something in Maria's tone that was a warning. 'What starts, Maria?'

'This is how she makes the trouble,' Maria said fiercely. 'She said that Susan stole one of her rings. Paolo offered to buy her another but, no, that was not good enough. She would go to the police if it wasn't returned. Poor Susan could not return it, could she, because she had not taken it in the first place. She did not want a bad...what do you call it? Recommend-ation?'

'Reference?'

Maria nodded distractedly. '*Si*. So she left. Louise had her way. And now it starts again.' There were tears in Maria's eyes. 'Take no notice, Jenna. *Per favore*. I do not want to lose you.'

Paul had advised her to take no notice as well. Surely Louise's preferences couldn't override them all? Jenna held Maria's gaze and tried to offer reassurance.

'I'm not going to let Louise drive me away with false accusations, don't worry.'

'I can't understand why she does this now,' Maria continued unhappily. 'It's not as if you and Paolo…' She paused, searching Jenna's gaze and then her eyes widened. 'Oh…' she murmured. 'Oh…*Dio mio!*'

But then she pinched Jenna's cheek. 'Take Ella to bed,' she advised calmly. 'I will see to dinner.'

Maria turned swiftly but not before Jenna caught the beginnings of what looked like a pleased smile.

She was not going to get away with it.

Not this time.

No way was Paul going to allow Louise to drive Jenna from his home.

His life.

No surprise that Louise suspected something might be brewing. Paul had never felt this kind of physical desire for any woman other than Jenna, and Louise was far from being stupid.

He had known that all along. He had been so confident he could ignore what his body was telling him—way back, that night in the paediatric ward's kitchen when he'd felt that insane desire to kiss Jenna's neck. He'd known what a mistake it would be to give in to that desire. It would have pre-empted another fiasco like the one that had surrounded the departure of Ella's last nanny. The needs of his family had to come first and Jenna being forced to leave would upset both Ella and his mother.

Of course, it had become rather more difficult after that night he'd met Jenna in the upstairs hallway wearing nothing but those short silky pants and a top that revealed far more than it covered, but even then he had been confident of controlling any hormonal urges.

What had happened this evening, in the bathroom? Seeing Jenna kneeling there, flushed and damp and laughing, with soap bubbles all over her face. Something had snapped. Quite painlessly. In fact, the rush of something warm and tender that was pure pleasure even before he'd tasted Jenna's lips had been a new experience.

The first step on a journey he knew he *had* to take. A voyage of discovery that Paul suspected would lead him somewhere he'd never been before. A curious mix of excitement and wariness bubbled within him so, no, it wasn't surprising that Louise had detected something different about him.

It also wasn't that surprising that Jenna had not made an excuse to escape the dinner and Louise's barely concealed fury. He had already witnessed Jenna's courage, hadn't he, when she had stood up to him and told him what she thought of his relationship with Danielle?

How things had changed since then!

A door Paul had never thought to try had swung open and he had fallen in love.

With a baby.

With Ella.

With having a family. His mother, Ella, Jenna and himself. To lose Jenna would change what had become a delight. As important in his life as his career.

Something to look forward to being a part of, every day.

Something that deserved all the protection he was capable of bestowing. Paul knew what the biggest threat was to this family unit. He forced himself to smile at Louise.

'More Chianti?' he offered.

'No.'

'Oh, go on, Lulu!' Gerald drained his wine-glass and held it towards the bottle Paul had picked up. 'Do you good. You need to loosen up a bit, pumpkin.'

Jenna followed Maria in from the kitchen. She had been quick to help collect the empty scallop shell dishes and tiny silver forks after their entrée and had earned an almost approving nod from Louise as she escaped the dining room.

Paul would have liked to escape as well. He hated formal rooms. The kitchen was where he should be eating.

In the heart of the household. With his family.

'Ossobuco,' Maria announced as Jenna care-fully placed a large, lidded earthenware dish on the table. 'One of my specialities.'

'Smells great,' Gerald enthused. 'Steak, huh?'

'Slow-stewed veal shanks,' Maria told him.

'It's like steak,' Paul murmured. 'You'll love it, Gerry.'

'No pasta for me.' Louise eyed a steaming bowl of ribbon pasta and sniffed the rich aroma of cheese. 'Just salad.'

'You'll fade away,' Gerald warned. 'And where would that leave me, gorgeous?' He blew a noisy kiss towards Louise and then grinned at Maria. 'Love of my life, this woman is,' he said firmly. 'Love of my life.' He leaned sideways to squeeze Louise's knee and she jumped visibly.

'*Gerald!* Not at the table, *please*!'

Paul tried to keep the sympathy out of his smile. If Gerald really did love Louise to such an extent, he was in for heartbreak.

Like mother, like daughter.

Although he was beginning to wonder if he had ever actually been really in love with Gwendolyn.

The thought distracted him enough to let the rest of this awkward meal pass without undue stress.

Was the degree to which you fell in love dependent, at least initially, on the level of physical attraction you felt for someone?

No. He couldn't allow that because if he did,

he would have to acknowledge that he was in real trouble right now. Physical attraction equated purely to lust.

The kind of lust he was feeling for Jenna.

It was almost unbearable to watch as she ate the delicious tiramisu Maria had made for dessert. The way she put the spoon in her mouth and then turned it upside down, obviously using her tongue to remove the chocolaty morsel…the dreamy look of pleasure that clouded her eyes…

A kind that far surpassed anything he'd ever felt in his life.

Yes. Any good intentions of staying well away from Ella's nanny had been blown completely out of the water. As though they had never even existed.

He would find a way to deal with Louise's displeasure.

He would *have* to.

The shared relief of seeing the front door close behind Louise and Gerald was not enough to justify the unusual serenity Maria was displaying.

Jenna eyed the older woman cautiously. Where was the concealed anxiety that would only dissipate when she had supervised the nightly blood-glucose test and dispensed reassurance?

'I might just pop upstairs and check on Ella,' she said casually. 'And then I'll help with the washing-up.'

'No, no!' Maria waved a hand airily. 'I can do that. By myself.'

The words were as casual as Jenna's but the significance of the hidden meaning was anything but.

'Are you sure?'

'*Si.*' Maria beamed at Jenna. 'If I need help, I'll call you.'

Jenna had to smile back. This was all part of her mission, wasn't it? For Maria to become independent and confident as far as managing her diabetes went?

'I'll get on with clearing up, then. It was a wonderful dinner, Maria.'

'*Molte grazie, cara.*' Maria stood on tiptoe to kiss Paul. 'You will help Jenna, yes?'

'Of course.'

It wasn't until Jenna's third trip from the dining room to the kitchen that she realised what Maria was up to. It wasn't that she had suddenly decided she was ready to manage her own testing and medications. She had taken this brave step because something was more important than her own nervousness. And that something was to encourage whatever she believed was happening between her son and Jenna.

She was forcing them to spend time together. Alone.

And it was working. Clearing the table wasn't difficult because they were moving, and loading the dishwasher was a breeze because Paul did it while Jenna took the linen to the laundry and wiped down the table, but the scallop shells and wineglasses needed to be washed by hand. They found themselves standing side by side in front of the huge old ceramic double sinks.

Paul rolled up his sleeves and watched as Jenna filled one of the sinks with hot water and added detergent. The moment she saw the soap bubbles begin to form she knew that washing these dishes was going to be an exercise in exquisite torture.

Jenna bent her head, allowing her loose hair to screen her face as she tried to concentrate on the task at hand. Maybe Paul wasn't feeling the same irresistible magnetic pull. Maybe that kiss in the bathroom had been a spur-of-the-moment thing and him saying that she belonged with him was just an example of the kind of Italian passion that had to be taken with a grain, or two, of salt.

Then again, maybe not.

Staring at the soap bubbles, Jenna could feel Paul staring at *her*.

Just like he had that night in the ward kitchen.

Like the start of that first fantasy she had had about him.

Only this was no fantasy. This was so real that every one of Jenna's senses were heightened. She could hear Paul's breathing as she hastily twisted the tap to close off the flow of water. She could feel the warmth from the nearness of his body and even smell the faintly musky aroma that reminded her exactly of what the taste of him on her lips had been.

When he lifted his hand to brush the hair screening the side of her face back, Jenna could feel each individual hair drag across her skin and the coolness as her neck was uncovered.

And then the warmth and sheer thrill of the

touch of Paul's lips on her neck as his hand cradled the back of her head. The dishcloth fell from Jenna's hand and a tiny sound of longing escaped her lips.

Did her head tilt back of her own volition or had it been due to the subtle pressure of the hand and lips that were blotting out anything other than a physical response?

It mirrored her fantasy so well it was confusing. As though she had stepped into a dream. Her throat was being kissed. She could feel the beat of her pulse against the tip of Paul's tongue, then his hands moving from her hair and coming to rest against her cheeks. He held her face gently, staring not at her mouth but into her eyes. A look that was not shuttered by him closing his eyes until the moment his lips claimed Jenna's.

This was nothing like that soft, questioning kiss in the bathroom.

That stepping over a boundary and discovering the taste of each other was over.

This was about an appetite unleashed. Passion that demanded satisfaction.

It was so smooth. The thrust of Paul's tongue

exploring her mouth, the stroke of his hands as they travelled down her back to cup her bottom and pull her closer. So smooth, it felt like flying.

Jenna was weightless. A leaf buffeted by the winds of desire. Her fingers were anchored in the waves of dark hair on Paul's head that felt almost as silky as Ella's. One of her breasts, the nipple painfully sensitised, pressed against the buttons of his shirt.

Until he broke the kiss and murmured something in Italian. Jenna couldn't understand the words but the tone was an invitation and Jenna would have agreed to anything Paul suggested at that moment. Her shaky smile became a gasp as Paul touched first one breast, and then the other, his fingers dragging slowly enough to send ripples of sensation that tugged sharply at something deep within Jenna.

She had to close her eyes and simply hang on then. Paul's hands slid beneath her top and the clasp of her bra sprang open. Jenna was hardly aware of leaning into his hands as they brushed a bare nipple. Of almost hanging from his neck as his leg nudged between hers, the rhythm of his rocking matched by the sweep and curl of his tongue against hers.

Paul broke the kiss and said something she couldn't catch.

'You're wet,' he said again.

Jenna started to blush. Who wouldn't be, with the magic Paul had been creating with his hands and mouth? But at the same moment she became aware of another sensation and it *was* a very wet one.

Warm water was trickling down her back. With the distraction she'd had when she'd turned off the tap, the fact that the movement had not been complete must have gone unnoticed. Water had continued to trickle into the sink Jenna was leaning back against and enough time had passed for the sink to fill and now overflow onto the tiled floor.

'Oh, no!'

'Non importa,' Paul soothed. He leaned behind Jenna to give the tap a firm twist. 'It doesn't matter.' He pulled her close again. 'Now, where were we, *cara*?'

His lips covered hers again but it wasn't the same. It *did* matter. Jenna could feel the puddle of water beneath her feet. Maria would not be happy when she came downstairs.

Or maybe she would share Paul's view that it didn't matter. Had she already come down to check on the clean-up operation and then stolen away because she had not wanted to interrupt what she had seen?

That idea bothered Jenna. The closeness of an Italian family was one thing but to have a relationship fostered because of maternal approval was something else.

And what if Maria had not come down yet?

Why not?

Had she run into problems with her blood-glucose monitor?

Was she alone in her bedroom, fretting but unwilling to interrupt what she *hoped* might be going on in her kitchen?

Paul pushed Jenna back far enough to see her face. 'What is it, *cara*? What's wrong?'

'Maria…'

'She has gone to bed. Don't worry.'

He pulled her into his arms again but Jenna was tense. Paul sighed and then frowned.

'Something *is* wrong, isn't it? Is Maria unwell?'

She should tell him. Jenna *wanted* to tell him but this just wasn't the right moment. It would drive him away because his family came first, and rightly so. But right now Jenna wanted him for herself, so badly.

Just for herself.

The battle in her head must be showing on her face. Paul was looking concerned now. She had to say something.

'I…don't think so but…but I should check. On Ella, anyway.'

Paul's frown deepened. He gave Jenna a searching look and then straightened, dropping his hands from her body. The mood was broken and Jenna was unhappily aware of her damp skirt and unfastened bra.

'We will both check,' Paul decided. 'On Maria and Ella.' With another frown—this time of concentration—he applied himself to the task of re-fastening the bra clasp but then he smiled wickedly. 'And then we will come back and finish what we have begun, yes?'

Jenna had to smile back. She knew he wasn't

talking about doing the dishes and when she was reassured about both Maria and Ella, there would be nothing to stop her surrendering completely to what she wanted more than she had ever wanted anything in her life.

With her hand firmly clasped in Paul's, she went with him from the kitchen and up the stairs. A light shone from beneath the door to Maria's bedroom but only silence greeted Paul's knock.

'She is asleep,' he predicted. 'I shall turn off her light.'

He opened the door and it took only a split second for Jenna to realise her fears had not been unfounded.

Maria lay slumped on the floor, fully dressed and apparently unconscious.

'*Dio!*' Paul was by her side in a moment, shaking his mother's shoulder. 'Maria? Can you hear me? What's wrong?'

Jenna knelt on the other side of Maria, feeling for her pulse. 'She's tachycardic,' she said a moment later. 'And clammy. I think she's hypoglycaemic.'

'Unlikely,' Paul snapped. 'She has type ll diabetes. It's a struggle keeping her levels down.'

'Not since she started insulin.'

Paul had tilted Maria's head back to protect her airway but his movements suddenly froze.

'What?'

'She...didn't want you to know. I've been helping her since I arrived but tonight she wanted to do her blood-glucose level by herself. She wasn't due for more insulin but if she took it by mistake...'

The look Paul was giving her was the coldest Jenna had ever seen. Much worse than when she had appeared in the emergency department with his daughter and had been blamed for at least contributing to the situation.

This time a member of his family was clearly in real danger and Jenna's responsibility was in no doubt.

Paul's order was terse. Just as cold as that look had been.

'Call an ambulance.'

CHAPTER EIGHT

THE calm efficiency of the paramedics was like balm in the face of Paul's ill-concealed level of tension.

They worked swiftly, gathering a case history while they started to assess and treat their patient, placing an oral airway, putting oxygen on, attaching ECG electrodes and taking baseline vital-sign measurements.

'How old is Maria?'

'Seventy-five,' Paul supplied. He was watching closely and Jenna knew he would be finding it difficult not to take charge of this assessment. He might be a doctor, but in this case he was also a relative and he needed to let the paramedics do their job.

'Pupils equal and reactive,' the female paramedic noted.

Jenna let her breath out consciously. At least this wasn't likely to be a stroke and no evidence of head injury had been found.

'And she's an insulin-dependent diabetic?'

'Apparently so.' Jenna could feel Paul's wrath in the clipped words like a physical blow.

'For how long?'

'About two months,' Jenna told the male paramedic.

'She's tachy at 120,' his partner said as she watched the screen of the life pack. 'Sinus rhythm.'

'When did she have her last dose of insulin?' The question was directed at Jenna rather than Paul, and she could actually feel the way he was trying to contain his frustration at not having the knowledge himself.

'Six p.m.'

'And she's eaten since then?'

'Yes,' Paul snapped.

'I'm not sure how much she ate,' Jenna said cautiously. 'It was a dinner party. I think Maria might have been more concerned about how much other people were eating.'

'Other medical conditions?'

'Hypertension,' Paul told him. 'She's on a beta-blocker. And osteo-arthritis. She takes high-dose aspirin.'

There was a moment's silence, in which the hiss of a deflating blood-pressure cuff could be heard, as the significance of Paul's statement sank in. Aspirin could trigger hypoglycaemia.

'She's not on aspirin any more,' Jenna said, almost reluctantly. No doctor would enjoy relaying inaccurate details but Paul would find this even more appalling. He hadn't known, had he? And this was his own mother. He must be cringing every time Jenna opened her mouth. 'Her GP changed her to another non-steroidal anti-inflammatory when she started the insulin.'

Jenna didn't dare risk looking at Paul.

'And she administers that herself?' The male paramedic was watching his partner insert an IV line. He took the cannula case from her and used the small amount of blood it contained to coat the tip of the test strip. The small blood-glucose monitor beeped as he slotted in the plastic strip.

'She's been doing her own blood-glucose

levels,' Jenna replied, 'but she still relies on me to do the insulin injections.'

'What was the last blood-glucose level?'

'I don't know,' Jenna admitted unhappily. She looked at Maria's dressing-table but the monitor was nowhere to be seen. How long had she and Paul been in the kitchen? Half an hour? She walked closer to the dresser.

The paramedics' monitor beeped. 'Low,' one of them noted. 'Shall I repeat it?'

'Yeah. I'll set up the giving set and dextrose.'

'Where's Maria's monitor?' Paul loomed behind Jenna. 'The last result will be in its memory.'

'She keeps it in here.' Jenna opened a small bottom drawer and moved a pile of neatly folded underwear.

'She keeps it *hidden*?'

Jenna swallowed. 'She didn't want you to know.'

'And the insulin?' Paul sounded dangerously calm. 'Where do you hide *that*?'

'In the nursery fridge.' Jenna had taken the small black case from the drawer. It clearly hadn't been used since dinner so Maria had had no warning that her levels had been dropping. If

Jenna had tested her earlier she might have been able to prevent this situation by giving oral glucose. The jar of jelly beans in the nursery were not there for Ella's benefit.

Paul snatched the case from Jenna's grasp and she kept her gaze down, looking at the top of the dresser as she heard the zip open. Even that sounded angry.

'Oh.' The exclamation was involuntary.

'What?' Paul demanded.

'There.' Jenna picked something up from among a collection of small perfume bottles. Crumpled silver foil.

Aspirin packaging.

'You said she wasn't taking aspirin any longer.'

'She's not supposed to.' Jenna steeled herself to look up and meet the fury in Paul's eyes. This was getting worse by the minute.

Or maybe not. The paramedics had been busy behind them and a cheerful female voice broke the tense silence hanging between Paul and Jenna.

'Maria? That's it, love. Open your eyes. Do you know where you are?'

As often happened, the administration of intravenous glucose had produced a miraculous result and Maria was going from being in a coma to full consciousness extremely rapidly.

'Who are you?' she demanded in a tone that reminded Jenna very much of her son. 'And what are you doing in my bedroom?'

'Maria!' Jenna's importance was dismissed as Paul swiftly knelt by his mother's side. *'Come sta?'*

A rapid-fire conversation in Italian followed. The paramedics exchanged a glance that conveyed both amusement at this unexpected development and satisfaction in a job well done. They began tidying up used packaging and equipment.

Jenna stayed where she was, beside the dresser, the little ball of crumpled foil in her clenched fist. Jenna recognised the word for aspirin in the conversation Paul was having with his mother and Maria looked both guilty and defiant. Then the tone changed and it was clear that they were arguing about something. Maria kept shaking her head and Jenna heard her name more than once. Paul was adamant in negating whatever

Maria was so determined about. Was she refusing transport to hospital?

The paramedics seemed to share Jenna's interpretation.

'Do you want us to take your mother to hospital?' one asked Paul.

'Of course,' he responded.

'No,' Maria said firmly. 'I want to stay here. Jenna will look after me.'

'*No,*' said Paul, even more firmly.

'It might be a good idea to go to the hospital for just a little while,' a paramedic suggested. 'Your blood-sugar levels will need careful watching for a bit.'

'Jenna can do that,' Maria insisted. She looked up. '*Scusi,* Jenna. I did not do the test. My hips were sore and I couldn't find my new pills and so I took the aspirin. I forgot I was not supposed to. *E colpa mia*…it is *my* fault.'

'No,' Paul said. 'It's not.'

'Of course it is, Paolo. I will not allow you to blame Jenna.'

The senior paramedic snapped the catches on his kit shut and looked at his watch.

'I will not be happy unless you go to the hospital, Maria. I want to make sure you are properly monitored.'

Maria looked from Paul to Jenna and back again. She had to be aware of how angry her son was and Jenna could almost hear the wheels turning as she tried to think of a way to defuse the situation.

'Very well,' she said finally. Almost regally. 'I will go to the hospital. For just a little while.'

The female paramedic came in with a carry chair to get Maria down the stairs and into the ambulance.

'I'm coming with you,' Paul announced. 'Jenna will stay with Danielle, of course.'

'Of course.' The weight of misery settled more heavily over Jenna thanks to the way Paul hadn't even bothered to make eye contact as they left.

And it continued to grow as she found herself in a house that was empty apart from herself and a soundly sleeping baby. Carrying the receiver for the baby monitor, Jenna paced, far too wound up to consider anything else.

How could things have changed so radically in

such a short time? Less than an hour ago she and Paul had been in a passionate embrace. On the point of making love.

Now he was not only absent physically, he had to be a million miles away from her emotionally, in the wake of discovering she had as good as deceived him about his mother's medical condition. And, worse, she had failed to live up to the responsibility she had taken on board by agreeing to keep it secret.

Sadly, he seemed to be automatically distancing himself from his daughter once more. Back to calling her Danielle instead of Ella.

Jenna finally stopped pacing and sat down. Just where she happened to be, which was at the foot of the staircase. She buried her face in her hands, too miserable to even cry.

From being at the point of virtually stepping through the finish flags on the mission Jenna had set herself by taking on this position, she felt like she had been picked up and rudely dropped right back at square one.

The chance of success had never seemed more remote.

* * *

Jenna was the picture of misery sitting there on the stairs.

She must have actually had her head in her hands but it was being lifted as Paul opened the front door and stepped back into his home.

Even from this distance, he could see how pale Jenna was. How huge and distressed her eyes were. It was suddenly much harder than he'd expected to stay angry with her.

'Is Maria all right?'

Paul nodded curtly. *No thanks to you,* the gesture said.

Jenna was getting to her feet and Paul noted with satisfaction her picking up the monitor on the stair beside her. At least she was attending to the responsibility of caring for Danielle. Then his gaze flicked back to the woman moving towards him. She seemed stiff, as though she had been sitting there for a long time. Waiting for him to come home? Surely not for the whole two hours he had been with Maria in the emergency department before they'd transferred her to an observation ward for the rest of the night.

'I'm sorry, Paul,' Jenna said. 'This shouldn't have happened.'

'You're damned right it shouldn't.' The door closed behind Paul with a bang.

Never mind that the ED consultant had reminded him how easy it was for an insulin-dependent diabetic to get hypoglycaemic. That sometimes the triggers couldn't even be identified and that it could happen when a dose of insulin precipitating the event might be identical to the previously normal dose. The fact that his mother had suffered this crisis was not what Paul was so angry about.

Not at all.

'You had *no* right,' he informed Jenna, 'to withhold this information from me. Maria is my *mother*. *I* am the one who should be supervising her medical care.'

A flash of something like understanding showed in Jenna's eyes. Possibly regret. But then her face tightened.

'I withheld nothing,' she responded. 'It was not my information to hand out and your mother asked me not to…repeatedly.'

Yes. His mother had said something along the

lines of Jenna wanting him to know. Saying how important it was. It was no excuse.

'And this was acceptable to you? To someone who has medical training and knows how serious any complications could be?'

'I… We seemed to be managing.'

'Seemed?' Paul sucked in his breath with a hiss. 'What does that mean? Has my mother run into problems like this before?'

Maria had denied it. Had said that Jenna was the perfect nurse.

An *angelo*. Paul was not to blame her.

'She's never lost consciousness.' Jenna was standing straighter, as though preparing to defend herself against whatever he chose to throw at her. 'Or even come close. She got a bit light-headed and wobbly once or twice when we first started. A bit diaphoretic on another occasion. Nothing that oral glucose couldn't reverse. I've kept a very careful watch on levels.'

'Not tonight, you didn't.'

'Your mother's starting to try and manage things herself. She knows I'm only going to be here to help her on a temporary basis.'

The reminder that Jenna intended to go back to her nursing position should have been a relief. Life would get back to normal.

Except that Paul didn't want the normality that had been his life before Jenna had come.

He didn't want her to leave.

'Maria insisted on doing her BGL by herself tonight. I thought she was being brave…that I should encourage her.'

They stared at each other. Paul was trying to remember. Maria had been insistent but it had been about something else. About checking on Ella.

Part of the subterfuge? Secret verbal signals? A loop that involved the safety of his family that he had been excluded from. By Jenna. A pact that had seen him lured into spending time alone with Jenna. In the kitchen.

Seducing the nanny.

Even now, the thought of that seduction and where it had inevitably been leading gave him a shaft of desire that cut through every other turbulent emotion Paul was dealing with. He pushed his reaction away with a vicious mental shove, but the effort was draining.

'I don't understand,' he said more quietly, 'why Maria didn't want me to know.'

'She…' Jenna took a deep breath. Sincerity was in every line of her face and there could be no doubting the truth of what she was about to say. 'She thought she would lose Ella. That you would think she wasn't physically capable of looking after her and that you would let Louise take her back to Auckland and raise her.'

Paul opened his mouth but no words came out. He was stunned. Did his mother really believe that he could have allowed her grandchild to be taken from her? To have her future removed? The reason the sun had truly begun to shine in her life again?

Just how much did Maria know?

Louise was being well paid to keep the secret. She wouldn't have told his mother.

Was it possible that he had been too late? That he had shut the stable door after the horse had bolted?

Did his mother believe that *she*, in fact, was protecting *him*?

This was disturbing. Easier to try and rewind

the conversation and focus on the anger he had brought home with him from the hospital where his mother still lay.

'This could have happened at any time,' he said coldly. 'What if you'd been out visiting that friend of yours? Anne, isn't it? What if you'd gone out and I hadn't known? Hadn't been able to check on Maria's glucose level? Hadn't been able to check on her before I went to bed?' He was distracting himself perfectly from any deeper issues now and the words were flooding out like machinegun fire. 'I would have found her tomorrow morning, would I not? *Dead!*' he finished aghast.

There. Let her try and defend herself now. He was more than ready for a good fight. Perhaps he needed one.

But to his dismay all Jenna's defence mechanisms clearly deserted her at that point. Hazel eyes filled with tears.

He was a brute, wasn't he? Why had he felt the attack so justified?

Oh, yes. He had wanted to blame someone because it had been so hurtful that his mother had kept her condition a secret from him. Had trusted Jenna more than her own son. She was family. *His* family. His to cherish and protect, and he'd been denied the opportunity.

And, yes, Jenna could have told him but she would have broken his mother's trust in her and the bond between these two women was of great importance to Maria. She adored Jenna. Since the arrival of Ella's new nanny, his mother had been happier and healthier than he had seen her in many, many years. He should be grateful to Jenna.

Instead, he had upset her with his harsh words. By his insinuation that her actions could have led to a fatal outcome. He had been too hard on her. She didn't deserve it.

Anger fled and Paul gave a soft groan.

'Ti prego, non piangere,' he said. 'Please, don't cry.'

He stepped closer, a hand outstretched instinctively to catch the tear that had just begun to roll down her pale cheek.

The moment he touched her, something else fled besides the anger. Any trace of barriers were simply swept away.

The frustration of having been interrupted in the kitchen.

The fear for his mother's safety.

The tension of the paramedics treating her.

The unexpected hours in the emergency department.

The anger and the hurt all coalesced into a surge of energy that demanded release.

Release that only this woman could give him.

Jenna closed her eyes at the touch of Paul's fingers on her cheek.

It wasn't soap bubbles he was stroking away this time but the evidence of sheer misery.

He had been so angry with her and yet now he was being so incredibly gentle.

Jenna had known, with absolute surety during that awful period of sitting on the stairs tonight, that she had come as close as she was ever going to come to making love with Paul Romano. A woman that had endangered a member of his family would never be acceptable in his bed. It was over, at least on his part.

Was it knowing that it would never happen that made her want it even more?

Or was this feeling of having the rug pulled from under her feet? To face Paul's wrath and now feel this gentle, *caring* gesture as he brushed away her tears?

Whatever.

Jenna had been transported from knowing that making love with this man was what she wanted more than she had ever wanted anything in her life to the sudden feeling that she might actually *die* if she didn't.

It was overwhelming. Confusing.

Frightening.

She snapped her eyes open, knowing that she would find the answer in the face that was now so close to her own.

An apology probably.

Or regret, perhaps.

Closure of some sort, anyway.

The answer was there, all right, in those eyes as dark as sin, but it wasn't an answer Jenna had been prepared for.

Opening her eyes had established a contact

that had flicked a switch and opened a connection as powerful as a lightning bolt.

Jenna was staring into a desire just as fierce as her own.

No words were needed to confirm what they both wanted.

What they *had* to have.

And as though they both knew the steps to this particular dance, Jenna's hands slipped around Paul's neck and he swept her into his arms and off her feet.

Jenna felt weightless in his arms as he took the stairs two at a time, not pausing until he was inside his own bedroom. A room Jenna had never seen before. She took in a momentary impression of a vast antique sleigh bed as Paul set her onto her feet and she placed the baby monitor on the beside table. She saw a blur of dark wood and rich burgundy drapes and sensed an aura that was purely masculine.

Somehow Jenna knew that she was the first woman to share this room with Paul and that knowledge increased a desire she wouldn't have believed could have become any stronger.

Jenna surrendered herself to that desire. She reached out, ready to be swept off her feet again and thrown onto the expanse of the bed beside them. To have her clothes ripped away and...

And it was nothing like that.

Slowly, carefully...almost reverently, Paul undressed her, caressing and kissing each new piece of her skin that was exposed.

Jenna tried to reciprocate, undoing the buttons of Paul's shirt and slipping her hands over his skin. Feeling the tight buds of his nipples and the iron-hard muscles beneath the satin surface of his body. But each of his new kisses made her pause, unable to do anything but revel in the touch of his hands and lips.

On her shoulders, her breasts, her waist... By the time Jenna was wearing only her knickers and Paul's fingers slipped beneath the elastic band, she was trembling all over, her fingers fumbling with his belt buckle.

'Please...' she whispered incoherently as her hands brushed the hardness below his belt.

Paul said something in Italian. A husky growl Jenna didn't understand, but it didn't matter.

The unbearable tension was broken as Paul took over the task she couldn't complete. He shed the rest of his clothes with startling swiftness and then Jenna was swept off her feet again and thrown onto the bed.

They were a tangle of limbs. Skin sliding on skin. Desperate to feed a hunger that only seemed to grow.

Until finally Paul was poised above Jenna. Between her legs. Her hands locked in his and held on either side of her pillow.

She was helpless. Totally vulnerable. Pinned by his gaze as much as by his body.

And she had never felt safer.

He entered her heart as completely as he did her body. Deeper with every thrust, and even as Jenna gave herself up to the ultimate physical satisfaction, a part of her knew she could never love any man as totally as she loved Paul Romano.

Heaven help her but her trust and her love had been won—probably at the moment he had touched her to brush away her tears.

And won absolutely.

CHAPTER NINE

THE alarm was set for 5.30 a.m.

Early enough for Paul to leave Jenna's apartment and creep upstairs to prepare for work in his own room as though nothing had changed in the Romano household.

'Do you think Maria knows what's going on?' Jenna turned back from checking the clock to find herself drawn very close to the man sharing her bed yet again.

'I don't think so.' Paul smoothed back Jenna's tousled hair and kissed her forehead. 'She is too excited about this new project of hers.'

'She is, isn't she? I think it's wonderful. She's managing so well now, isn't she? I think that night in the hospital and the extra tests and new management plan have given her a whole new lease on life. Did I tell you that her medic-alert bracelet finally arrived today?'

'I hope she is going to wear it. She's still being stubborn about telling Louise.'

'She's wearing it already. Didn't you notice at dinner?'

'No.'

'Maybe Louise won't notice either.'

'She'll notice.'

'Mmm.' Bed wasn't the place to be thinking about Louise Gibbs or the unpleasantness she would undoubtedly create when she learned that Paul and Jenna had embarked on a passionate affair that showed no signs of burning out. 'Anyway, I think this new idea of Maria's is fantastic. I'm sure her recipe book will be a huge success.'

'I'm not so sure.'

'But her cooking's fabulous!'

'That's the problem.' Paul kissed Jenna's nose. 'I think we might all get very fat, tasting all this new food she keeps creating.'

'Mmm.' Jenna smiled as Paul's lips covered hers. A lingering kiss that spoke of familiarity and sheer pleasure. A moment later her tone was mischievous. 'So, you think I'm getting fat, then?'

'Let me see!'

Jenna giggled as Paul threw back the covers but then she stilled as she felt Paul's gaze roam her body.

'You are *fantastica*,' he murmured. *'Perfetta!'*

His hand traced the route his gaze had taken, lightly stroking Jenna's breast, trailing over her belly and then sliding over the curve of her hip. He drew her even closer and Jenna felt desire spiral again, as so often happened when they should have been lulled into satiated sleep in the wake of passion.

It seemed that neither of them could get enough of the other. That each time they made love it was just another taste of something much bigger. Part of a feast that could still not begin to assuage a mutual appetite. Whenever Jenna thought their physical relationship couldn't possibly get any better, Paul would discover some new place she loved to be touched. Or a new location—like the shower. Or he would change the pace.

Or just hold her and she would fall asleep in his

arms aware of nothing other than the sheer bliss of his presence and warmth and the astonishing capacity she was discovering that he had to be both fierce and gentle at the same time.

He was holding her now. Neither of them were ready to sleep but Paul's outward breath sounded like a sigh. Jenna touched his cheek.

'You're tired.'

'It's been a long day.'

'How did the meeting with Louise go?'

'As well as could be expected. She cried a lot but Gerry was there to hold her hand.'

'It's a shame that there will always be a cloud over celebrating Ella's birthday. That…it's the day her mother died.' Jenna's words were tentative. By tacit consent, until now, they had never really discussed Gwendolyn.

Had they created a bubble? An unreal kind of space that was floating among the stuff of real life—still unnoticed thanks to their discretion?

If so, it was quite a tough bubble because it had lasted nearly a month already and seemed to get stronger every day. And, like a bubble, it seemed to spread a little magic into real life.

Things other than the bed Paul chose to sleep in when he was not on call were changing. He left for the hospital a little later in the mornings and he was managing to get home a little earlier some days. When he had time off at the weekends, he surprised his small family by suggesting outings. To the beach and the wildlife park and even an open-air opera in the city's huge central park, which had his mother sighing happily for days afterwards.

It was not just their physical relationship that was going from strength to strength. Paul and Jenna were sharing the joy of watching Ella develop. A bond that made them…almost…a real family. Jenna suspected Maria must have a very good idea of what was going on under her roof but she had also chosen discretion. To maintain a new—and wonderful—status quo, perhaps?

Had Jenna risked pricking the bubble by mentioning Ella's real mother?

Apparently not.

'It's only this first anniversary of Gwen's death that needs to be commemorated,' Paul said. 'It will be enough. It's time to put the past behind us.'

Jenna took a deep breath, encouraged enough to ask something that had begun to taunt her.

'Do you miss her very much?'

'Gwen?' Paul was silent for a moment. 'I think of her often,' he admitted finally. Heavily. 'How can I not, with Ella here to remind me?'

Jenna was silent, too. Of course he would remember. Every day. How could she ever hope to compete with such a ghost?

Paul seemed to sense her doubt. His hold on her tightened. 'Does it bother you, *tesoro*?'

'I am a little jealous.' Jenna tried to keep her tone light-hearted. Paul could just laugh at her if he wished. But he didn't.

'There's no need to be,' he said. 'You are as different from Gwendolyn as…as chalk and cheese. How I feel about you is nothing like how I felt about Ella's mother.'

His tone and touch were reassuring. And surely no one could kiss like this if they weren't in love? But Jenna needed more. She wanted to hear the words.

'But you were in love with Gwendolyn, weren't you?' she asked quietly.

'Totally,' Paul agreed. 'And she was clever. She refused to sleep with me before marriage. I was obsessed. I had no choice.'

Jenna's heart sank. He had a choice now. She had given herself—completely—without asking for even a hint of commitment. Had she made a terrible mistake?

'It didn't last, of course,' Paul continued evenly. 'The infatuation wore off and there was little else there. If it hadn't been for the baby I'm quite sure the marriage would not have lasted. It *couldn't* have lasted.'

'Oh…' Jenna absorbed the surprising information that the marriage had not been so perfect after all.

And Paul had said she was nothing like Gwendolyn.

Chalk and cheese.

That was a *good* thing, then. She cuddled closer, extending sympathy in her touch but also a promise. They had far more than a physical infatuation. They had something that *could* last. For ever. She didn't need to rush anything. Ask for anything Paul wasn't ready to give. He had been manipulated by a woman once before and Jenna was certainly not going to make the same mistake.

'We have arranged a short church service on the actual day of the anniversary,' Paul said then. 'It's best that we have Ella's party on a Saturday, anyway, because that way I can be here to enjoy it all.'

'It will be fun.' It was a relief to turn to a subject they both loved. 'I think Ella's excited.'

'She is always excited. Every day is a new adventure for that little one.'

'She's doing so well, isn't she? Almost walking properly and I'm sure she learns a new word every day.'

Paul chuckled. 'I hear "No!" more than anything else. And I'm not sure I approve of this foot-stamping.'

Jenna grinned. 'She takes after her father.'

Oddly, her words created an instant tension in Paul's body.

'What do you mean by that?'

'Just that she knows what she wants and how to get it.' Jenna twisted in Paul's arms. 'Are you offended?'

She felt him relax. 'No. Of course not. But I told you her mother was an expert in getting what she wanted.'

And Jenna had reminded him. Stupid. It seemed to have changed something in the intimate atmosphere of their private time. Paul seemed withdrawn. Lost in his own thoughts. Jenna propped herself up on one elbow and bend down to drop a brief, gentle kiss on his lips.

'You're not getting sick of this, are you?'

'Of being here? With you? What a ridiculous notion!' Paul buried his fingers in the tousled waves of Jenna's hair, holding her head as he kissed her properly, but he sighed again when they broke apart to draw breath.

'It is getting a little tiresome,' he admitted, 'sneaking around my own house in the dark like some kind of burglar. I think it's time we stopped trying to be so discreet.'

Jenna caught her breath. 'You want to tell people? *Louise?*' If he was prepared to weather that storm, it could only be taken as a kind of commitment to a future, couldn't it?

'Not yet,' Paul said cautiously. 'Not until this

memorial service is over with. When we can all put the past behind us and start again. We will remember and then we will celebrate Ella's birthday and then…' He kissed Jenna once more. 'Then there will be no need to tiptoe around the feelings of others. We will enjoy our time together without hiding from anyone.'

Our time together.

How long would it be?

There was a letter sitting near the clock on Jenna's bedside table. A query from her old hospital in Dunedin asking her to confirm whether she intended to return to her position because the woman currently filling it was keen to continue on a permanent basis.

The halfway point of Jenna's intended stay with the Romano family as their nanny had come and gone. Her time with Paul could be running out and it was difficult not to think about it when the need to respond to the letter was gaining urgency.

She couldn't broach the subject yet, however. Not this week, in the run-up to the memorial service and then the party. As Paul had said, the anniversary marked the end of a period most would consider appropriate for mourning. With a new start and especially with the plan to bring their relationship into the open, the opportunity to discuss the future would naturally present itself.

Their future.

Jenna wasn't going to rush anything. It was far too precious to risk.

Danielle Romano's first birthday party might have been toned down enough to acknowledge the more sombre aspects of the date, but it was still enough of a production to be a blaze of colour.

The house was a rainbow of helium balloons. The dining-room table was covered with bite-sized treats and a gorgeous birthday cake Maria had created that looked exactly like Ella's favourite toy, Letto the rabbit. Brightly wrapped parcels dominated the lounge and Ella was a princess, wearing a gorgeous white smocked dress and with silver ribbons adorning the ends of two miniature black pigtails. She had knee-high white socks with a ruffle of lace on the top, but she was flatly refusing to keep shoes on her feet.

'No!' she pronounced yet again, hurling one

shoe and then the other back at Louise while the photographer waited patiently to try and get a family shot.

'Give it a rest, Lulu,' Gerald advised. 'Nobody'll notice.' He grinned at Paul. 'Not too early for a spot of bourbon, is it, mate?'

'But the photo!' Louise protested. 'I want it to be special.'

As special as the one of Gwendolyn, perhaps, that Louise had insisted be placed beside the cake on the dining table. They had all trooped in to admire the feast earlier and Ella had been awestruck by her cake.

'*Letto!*' she had said joyously. The grandmothers had smiled proudly at yet another addition to an expanding vocabulary.

Louise had picked up the photograph beside the cake. 'It's your mummy,' she had reminded Ella. 'Can you say "Mummy", darling?'

And Ella had almost obliged. '*Mum*—ma!'

She wasn't being so obliging now, however and for once Maria was in agreement with Louise. 'Wear the shoes, *cara*,' she begged. 'Just for one photo.'

'No!' Ella said. And grinned.

Jenna watched as both grandmothers tried to buckle a small shoe onto each of Ella's feet.

'What is that?' Louise suddenly asked. 'What *are* you wearing, Maria?'

'Just an alert bracelet.' Maria's tone was deliberately offhand but not very successful. The undertone of significance was unmistakable and she seemed unable to prevent the anxious glance she cast at Paul, who was pouring a drink for Gerald.

'What's it for?'

'My diabetes, that's all.'

'But why wear a bracelet?'

'It's in case someone finds you unconscious in the street,' Gerald said helpfully. 'You've seen the one I've got one for my dodgy ticker.' He leered and Jenna and lowered his voice to a stage whisper. 'It's the only thing I *never* take off, y'know.'

Jenna didn't want to know. She caught Paul's gaze and they exchanged a look of complete understanding.

'I didn't think your diabetes was that serious.' Louise seemed to have forgotten her mission with Ella's shoes. 'I mean, you don't have to have injections for it or anything, do you?'

'I do now,' Maria said reluctantly. 'There. Shoes on!' The distraction was clearly welcome. 'Let's get a picture quickly before they come off again.'

The family was positioned on a couch. Gerald and Jenna watched from behind the photographer who had a squeaky, rubber toy to catch Ella's attention and make her smile. Paul held his daughter who was holding Letto and had a grandmother sitting on either side. Three generations of Romanos, with the same dark hair and eyes. The same smile. Louise looked like an outsider, with the blue eyes and blonde hair she had passed on to her own daughter, but she wasn't, was she? She was as much a part of this unusual family portrait as anyone else. It was herself and Gerald who were the outsiders.

Paul was smiling at Jenna as the shutter clicked and then clicked again but, strangely, it made her feel more excluded. She was reminded of that very first time she had been in the same space as this group—when Paul had arrived home in time to conduct the interview for the position as Ella's nanny. It seemed such a long time ago.

Had anything really changed?

Maria still had an anxious air and Louise still emanated determination to stake her claim and an almost smug appreciation of her power.

And Jenna felt no closer to understanding the missing link but there could be no doubt that something fundamental *had* changed. Ella was looking up at her father. She stretched out a small hand and touched his face and he was smiling back at her. He murmured something in Italian that made Ella smile and then he bent his head and pressed a kiss to the smooth hair at the top of one pigtail.

'Yes!' the photographer enthused. 'That's lovely!'

And it was. If nothing else, Jenna had succeeded in what she'd set out to do with this interim period in her life. She had helped create and then cement a bond between a father and a daughter. Paul was not going to stop loving Ella, whether or not Jenna was part of their lives in the future.

'We need a photograph with Jenna as well,' Maria decreed. 'Come and sit, Jenna!'

The brilliant smile Louise had turned on repeatedly for the photographer vanished. 'These are *family* photographs,' she said with deliberate clarity.

'*Si.*' Maria nodded her agreement. 'And Jenna is part of the family.'

Louise turned her head with even more deliberation. 'There's hardly room on the couch, is there?'

'Mmm.' Paul was also in agreement. 'You could swap places with Jenna for this one, Louise.'

The photographer and Gerald were the only people slow to catch on to the subtle way Louise froze. The ice in the atmosphere. The stare Jenna was subjected to was calculating. Louise was weighing her options. Quite unexpectedly, the boundary Jenna had known would have to be approached was visible. Were Paul and Maria ready to step over it or were they missing the significance of what they were suggesting?

Louise was missing nothing and she looked as though she would simply refuse. Create a scene that could well ruin the celebration of Ella's birthday. But she was undecided. Confused, perhaps, over the significance of the desire to include Jenna? Was she just a much-appreciated employee? Or something more dangerous?

Jenna felt a moment of panic. This wasn't the time. She wasn't ready. She opened her mouth to demur but instinctively she caught Paul's gaze for an instant.

Was he choosing this moment to make a statement about the future?

If so, Jenna had to feel sorry for Louise because, while it was Ella's birthday and a chance to celebrate life and the possibility of happiness in the future, it was also very close to the anniversary of the death of this woman's daughter.

Of Paul's wife.

The undercurrents swirled more strongly than they ever had. Maybe Paul was simply asking for Jenna's support to get through a difficult time and his needs had to take priority over those of his mother-in-law.

So did Maria's. Her gaze was pleading. Was she ready and willing to support anything her son wished to do in the name of his future happiness but didn't want to rush Jenna?

Whatever the motivations, both Maria and Paul wanted her there beside them. They wanted a record of Jenna's presence. On this occasion and as part of their family.

Out of nowhere, the words that Paul had spoken once before echoed in Jenna's mind.

'You belong,' he'd said. *'With me.'*

And she did. Jenna returned her gaze to meet that of Louise and she took a deep breath and straightened her spine.

And after what seemed an interminable pause, Gerald saved the day.

'Come on, Lulu. Let me pour you a glass of bubbly.'

Louise conceded. She rose and walked with dignity to where Gerald had taken charge of the drinks on the sideboard. She accepted the flute of champagne and drank it with her back turned to the group on the couch as the photographer squeaked the toy again and took another volley of shots.

Then Maria stood up. 'I would like champagne, too,' she announced. 'This is a *compleanno*, is it not? A birthday!'

'Gotcha.' Gerald winked. 'Coming right up!'

So Paul and Jenna and Ella were left on the couch and the session seemed to be over. Ella was getting bored. She pulled off her detested shoes and then climbed to her feet on Paul's lap. Paul held her securely around her waist as she leaned toward Jenna.

'*Mum*-ma!' Ella crowed happily.

Jenna caught Paul's gaze, horrified, but he simply smiled with only a hint of resignation.

'*Nice,*' the photographer murmured, the shutter clicking again.

'Oh…my…God,' Louise breathed. She drained her glass and set it down soundlessly on the sideboard. Then she turned and walked through the open French doors and into the garden.

'Lu?' Gerald watched in bewilderment. 'You all right, babe?' He hurriedly refilled the flute and topped up his own glass then followed Louise outside.

The photographer was scrolling through his shots. 'These are great,' he said. ' You want a break before we start on the presents or do you want to do the cake next?'

'Let's have a break,' Maria said. 'Come with me to the kitchen and I'll get you some coffee. You must try my *biscotti*.'

'Sounds good.'

'My cooking is always good,' Maria said serenely. 'Come! I wish to discuss the photographs with you. Tell me, have you ever taken pictures of food? For a recipe book?'

'Oh, dear,' Jenna said into the new silence. She gazed sadly at Ella's small face. 'You have no idea what you've done, have you, sweetheart?'

'*Mum*-ma,' Ella said again. She bounced on Paul's knee and then climbed into Jenna's arms to hug her.

'I'm sorry,' Jenna said to Paul over Ella's shoulder. 'I don't know what to say. This must be upsetting for you as well as Louise.'

'Why?' Paul sounded unperturbed. 'Ella has never known her birth mother. You are the closest thing to a mother she's ever had.'

And maybe that wasn't a good thing. She was too involved. With everybody here. It was a recipe for heart break.

'But I'm not…I'm not even going to be here for much longer.' She hadn't wanted to be the one to initiate a discussion about their future but it was going to happen whether she liked it or not.

'You have another three months before you can even think about returning to your nursing position,' Paul pointed out. 'A lot can happen in three months, *bella*.'

'I may not last the three months,' Jenna said ruefully, giving Ella another cuddle. 'I suspect Louise is really on the warpath now.'

'This has nothing to do with Louise. She will just have to accept things the way they are. I'll deal with it.' Paul smiled and tweaked the end of Ella's pigtail. 'We can't let you leave, you know. You're far too important to all of us.'

Jenna's smile was as wobbly as the pulse she could feel beating in her throat. They had started so they might as well finish this.

'I can't stay for ever.'

'Why not?'

That pulse skipped a beat. 'I'm not really a nanny,' Jenna said carefully. 'I never intended leaving my nursing career for good. You know that.' Ella wriggled in her arms impatiently and Jenna let her slide down to the floor.

'Who said you had to?' Paul watched Ella's fast crawl towards the pile of gifts. 'We could work something out. If you took a nursing position here, we could all work around your shifts. Maria is so much better now and she would be delighted to help. If you did night shifts, *I* could help.' He caught Jenna's hand. 'We could employ a nanny.'

Jenna had to laugh. 'What? Employ a nanny? *For* a nanny? That would be crazy.'

Paul was silent for a moment. '*Si,*' he agreed then. 'It would not work, would it?'

Jenna's heart sank even as she felt Paul's fingers curl around her own with a more intense grip.

'But...' Paul seemed to be waiting to catch Jenna's gaze and his tone gave no clue as to the words he was about to utter. 'What if I was employing a nanny to help my *wife*?'

'I...don't understand,' Jenna said hesitantly. But that wasn't entirely true, was it? Jenna could practically feel the blood fizzing in her veins as the implication of Paul's words sank in.

'Ella loves you,' Paul said softly. 'You are her "*Mum*-ma".'

Jenna held her breath. Was he finally going to say it? But the suspense was too much and she had to break the short silence herself.

'You're proposing to me? Because you want to keep Ella's nanny?'

'No.' Paul's grip tightened on her hand to the extent it was almost painful. 'I am proposing to you because I love you, Jenna. I want you to be my wife. To stay in my life. To be a part of my family…for ever.'

'But…what about Louise?'

Paul raised an eyebrow. 'This is between you and me, *cara*. Louise will have to accept it.'

Jenna swallowed hard. 'Maybe it's too soon. It's only been a year since…'

'It's not too soon. This is a new start. And, like I told you, the way I feel about you is nothing like how I felt about Gwendolyn. Chalk and cheese, remember?'

Jenna nodded. Of course she remembered. Paul's smile was as reassuring as his kisses had been in bed the other night. *Loving.* His eyes begged for understanding.

'I want to start living again. I want *you*, Jenna, and if you are my wife, Louise will have no choice but to accept it. Say yes, *carissima*. Say you'll marry me.'

Did the undercurrents matter? That he wasn't in love with her the same way he had been with Gwendolyn? That Jenna's relationship with Ella might be the precipitating factor? He'd said it, hadn't he?

He loved her.

The kiss Paul pressed to her lips was so tender. So sincere. So full of promise that Jenna had no difficulty allowing joy to smother any doubts.

'I...love you, too, Paul,' she whispered as they broke the kiss. 'More than I thought I could ever love anyone.'

'So you'll marry me?'

'Of course I will.'

He kissed her again but Jenna was too conscious of those open French doors and the couple that could walk back into the room at any moment.

'Is now the time?' she wondered aloud.

'We are celebrating today. We have remembered and agreed to put sadness behind us. What better time to make a new start?'

Jenna couldn't help a fearful glance towards the doors. Gerald's voice was becoming louder.

'Time for a top-up,' they heard him say. 'Come on, Lulu. Chin up, babe!'

Paul chuckled. 'Gerald might be a godsend when it comes to dealing with Louise,' he said thoughtfully. 'I will speak to her later today. When the party is over.' He stood up and drew Jenna to her feet. 'For now, let me get us both some champagne. We will toast our future.' His smile said everything Jenna could have wished to hear. 'Our love.'

CHAPTER TEN

THE presents had been opened and nobody minded that Ella had been more interested in the bows and wrapping paper.

Paul had been the one to hold Ella up and help blow out the candle on the 'Letto' cake and the photographer left the gathering as they did their best to taste every special food Maria had created for the occasion.

It was one very tired baby that Jenna finally took upstairs to bathe and get ready for bed.

The nod from Paul when he had given Ella a goodnight kiss had been accompanied by what seemed a significant glance.

The party is over, it said. *I haven't forgotten that I'm going to talk to Louise.*

Jenna could think of little else as she quickly bathed Ella and dried her and dusted her with sweet-smelling talcum powder. She prepared the formula and while it warming she tidied a few things around the nursery. Humming a song for Ella, Jenna dimmed the lights and switched on the baby monitor so she wouldn't forget and have to come upstairs again. The unit she kept with her in the evenings was downstairs somewhere. Paul would know where it was. He'd taken it with him that morning in case Ella woke up while Jenna was in the shower.

The microwave beeped and it wasn't until Jenna sat down in the armchair with Ella and the bottle of milk and stopped singing that she became aware of the voices.

'Don't you dare walk out on me, Louise.'

It was Paul's voice and the controlled fury she could hear made Jenna's jaw drop. She looked down but Ella seemed unperturbed. She insisted on hanging onto her bottle with both hands for this supper drink now. Jenna could put her into her cot to drink it but she was loath to give up this last cuddle of the day.

She would have to disturb Ella to get up and switch the channel on the monitor so it wasn't broadcasting two ways but the baby's eyes were drooping already. She'd be asleep in a very short space of time and Jenna could attend to the channel as soon as she'd put Ella into her cot.

'We're going to settle this,' she heard Paul say. 'For good.'

'It's already settled. You can't break your promise, Paul.'

'You made a promise, too, Louise. Remember? Or am I not paying you enough to keep remembering?'

Jenna's eyes widened. She shouldn't be listening to this. She *shouldn't*.

'You promised you wouldn't marry. That you wouldn't repl—'

'Actually, I said I had no intention of marrying again,' Paul cut in. 'And I didn't at the time. Things change.'

'I can't believe you've fallen for the nanny, Paul. Can't you see what a cliché it is?'

'I haven't *fallen* for Jenna. I might have made that mistake with your daughter, Louise, but that's never going to happen again. That's one promise I'll have no trouble keeping. Maria adores Jenna. So does Danielle. She has become a part of the family and my family matters to me above all else. I will do whatever is within my power to make them happy, and that includes marriage to Jenna. It is *not* negotiable.'

Jenna had to press a hand against her mouth.

To cover the soft sound of distress that would have been impossible to repress.

A cry of pain. Jenna knew it was a physical impossibility but she could swear she actually felt her heart break. A kind of tearing sensation that left a dreadful ache behind it.

Paul might want her but he didn't really love her, did he? Not the way she loved him. He hadn't fallen in love with her at all. How could she have missed that realisation? He had told her as much himself, hadn't he? When he'd said that how he felt about her was completely different to how he'd felt about Gwendolyn.

Chalk and cheese.

To be in love. And to *not* be in love.

It was so true that eavesdroppers never heard anything about themselves that they might want to hear. Jenna had no desire to hear any more of this conversation. What she wanted to do was run. To run and hide somewhere like a wild animal. To find a private place to lick her wounds. But the blow she had just received felt mortal and any strength had deserted her.

Paul wasn't in love with her. He was doing this for his mother. And his daughter.

It was not negotiable. And it could never be enough. Not for Jenna.

Ella had fallen asleep in her arms. She should take her over to her cot but she couldn't move. Jenna was totally numb. Reeling with the shock of what she had just overheard.

She might not want to hear any more of the dreadful conversation taking place downstairs somewhere—presumably in the library that doubled as Paul's office.

But she had no choice.

Jenna sat there, holding Ella, with tears streaming down her face. She found herself rocking gently, not for the baby's benefit but for her own.

It seemed the only way to try and deal with the pain.

She was only half-aware of the voices she

could still hear. Carefully controlled fury in both of them. They did not want to be overheard. Paul would have no idea at all that he'd left the monitor in there. Had he gone in early to check his emails perhaps? He had far more important things on his mind than anything that might be lying around his office.

It didn't matter any more that Jenna was eaves-dropping because she couldn't possibly hear anything more shocking than she already had.

'You can't just replace Danielle's mother,' Louise said.

'She never *had* a mother. Not until Jenna came.'

A sound of outrage came from Louise. 'You did make a promise, Paul. You said that you would bring Danielle up to know how special her mother was. How is she going to know that if she thinks some gold-digging *nanny* is her mother?'

'I'm sure you'll remind her.'

'Oh…I *will*,' Louise said viciously. 'I'll do more than that. I'll get custody and she'll grow up with me. She'll grow up knowing exactly how special her *real* mother was.'

'Special? Oh, come on, Louise. She was just

like you. Only interested in the prestige that money can buy.'

'How dare you?' Louise snarled.

'Oh, I dare.' The words were pure ice. 'And don't even think about trying for custody, Louise.'

'You know I'd get it. I'm the only blood relative Danielle has.'

It took a few seconds for the words to penetrate the mist of misery Jenna was in. She blinked, clearing the tears from her eyes. With a huge effort she pushed through the wall of pain surrounding her. She shook her head. If she listened more carefully she would realise she had not heard what she thought she'd just heard.

'And not as far as my mother is concerned. Ella is her granddaughter and I will simply not allow you to suggest otherwise.'

'*Suggest*! It's fact and you and I both know it. I think it's time Maria knew the truth.'

The truth? Jenna's jaw had dropped. This was incomprehensible. It was blatantly obvious that Ella was Paul's daughter. Did he really believe she wasn't?

It fitted, though, didn't it? It was the missing

piece of the puzzle. The explanation of why Paul had failed to bond with a motherless baby. The cause of the marriage being less than perfect. The reason Louise had had an aura of power in this household. But if Paul wasn't Ella's father, why had he allowed everyone to think he was? Simply for the sake of his mother? Was family *that* important?

Maybe he knew at a subconscious level what Jenna had known from the first moment she had seen them together. The same hair and eyes. That same smile that began with a crinkle around their eyes. There was no way Ella could be anyone else's child. Jenna knew because she could see the similarities.

Because she loved them. Both of them.

The overpowering strength of that love was enough to send a new wave of pain through her body. Paul didn't feel the same way. And if he was capable of pretending a child was his own when he didn't believe that was true, for the sake of his mother, then it was far less a leap of the imagination that he could marry someone for a similar purpose.

Had it all been a calculated act? Even the way he had made love to her?

She had missed something being said below. It was hard to refocus.

'Go home, Louise,' Paul was saying wearily. 'Before you say something you'll really regret. One word from you and I'll ruin you. Do you really think I'd let you take Danielle back to the kind of lifestyle you raised your own daughter in? You're a lot older now, Louise. How many men do you think are going to be happy to keep paying for your services?'

'I hate you,' Louise spat.

'*Non importa.* It makes no difference to me. I will not, however, allow you to harm my family.'

'I don't need you. I don't need your money. I have Gerald now. He'll look after me.' Louise sounded almost desperate. 'He'd pay any legal expenses if I decide to go for custody.'

'You think he'll still be happy to pay when he learns that the "love of his life" is after nothing more than his money?'

'Don't you *dare* say that about me!'

'It's the truth. You have no real morality. I think

Gerald would be very upset to learn the truth. I can assure you that my marriage to your daughter would never have taken place if I'd known how like you she really was.'

Paul seemed to be pacing in the library because his voice was getting fainter. Or did he have his hand over his face, Jenna wondered, in a gesture of utter weariness?

His words became clearer. 'Sitting there at that farce of a service the other night made me almost ill, do you know that? The tributes to the excited mother-to-be. The loving *wife*.'

Jenna remembered that conversation she'd had with Anne. Gwendolyn hadn't been popular, had she? Her friend had been very perceptive. The idea of how perfect Ella's mother had been had only come through Louise.

Louise was obviously a master in using attack as a form of defence. Jenna actually gasped aloud at her next words.

'If Gwen had to go elsewhere to find satisfaction, whose fault is that, Paul?'

'Get out of my house, Louise.'

'You can't stop me seeing my granddaughter. *My* granddaughter. She's no relative of yours.'

'My mother is, however, and I will not allow you to damage her life. I will claim Ella as my child. She *is* my child now, thanks to Jenna.'

'You won't get away with this. I will not allow you to marry Jennifer.'

'You have no choice, Louise. None at all.'

Louise might not have a choice but Jenna did.

While it would break her heart to leave this house, that was exactly what she was going to have to do.

The very thought of leaving was so awful that Jenna couldn't allow herself time to think about it. It was a cut that would have to be made swiftly—before she could change her mind.

Tears were already threatening as she gently laid the sleeping Ella in her cot. What if she never saw this child that she loved so much again?

Or Maria?

Leaving Maria would be almost like losing another mother, and there was no way she could explain the real reason for leaving, was there?

Not without telling Maria what she had accidentally overheard.

What if she was wrong? What if the similarities to Paul were simply coincidence because Ella's *real* father happened to have the kind of genes that could bestow that dark colouring?

She could understand Paul's determination not to destroy his mother's happiness. There was no way she could do it herself.

Did Maria have any idea of how much her son loved her? The lengths he was prepared to go to in order to make her happy? Jenna already knew he was a man capable of great passion but she'd had no idea of the scope that could encompass. He could live a lie perfectly convincingly if he felt the need. Even if he didn't know he *was* living one.

Jenna couldn't do that.

There was no way she could give herself in marriage to a man she loved and then pretend that everything was perfect. That he loved her as much as she loved him.

Not when she knew he didn't. When she knew the real reason he was prepared to do it.

Every second that passed, every new thought and emotion that assailed Jenna was going to make this harder. With a final touch of Ella's silky curls Jenna fled the nursery and ran downstairs.

The door to the library was open now and there was no sound of any voices. The door to the lounge was closed and Jenna slipped past. Through the kitchen and into her apartment.

An overnight bag was all she needed for the moment. Anne would be happy to give her a bed for a night or two until she could decide what to do next. It took only minutes to fill and it wasn't heavy.

Nothing would ever feel as heavy as the emotional weight Jenna was carrying as she made her way back through the kitchen and into the hallway. It would have been much easier to let herself out through the separate entrance to the apartment but Jenna knew she would have to find Paul and explain why she was leaving.

At least she was finally too numb to feel any new pain.

And then she stepped from the kitchen into the

hallway just as Paul stepped through the door to the lounge, and she knew she had been wrong.

She *could* feel new pain.

That smile. That look in his eyes as he caught her gaze.

'I was just coming to look for you,' he said. 'I've talked to Louise.'

Jenna's mouth was dry. 'I know. I heard you. You must have left the baby monitor in your office, Paul. It wasn't intentional but I overheard part of what you said.'

Paul's smile faded but he didn't seem to be listening to what Jenna was saying. He was too eager to speak again himself.

'All's well, *carissima*. It's all sorted.'

'No, Paul.' Jenna tried to swallow but couldn't. 'It's not.'

He frowned, his gaze sliding downwards. 'What is that? Why do you have a bag?'

'I'm leaving,' Jenna said simply. 'I can't stay, Paul. I can't…marry you.'

'What do you mean, you *can't* marry me? I don't understand.'

'You didn't tell me the truth.'

Paul's frown deepened. He cast a glance over his shoulder to check that he'd closed the door to the lounge. 'How much did you overhear?'

'Enough. I know that you think Ella is not your daughter.'

'She isn't! But—'

Jenna gave an incredulous huff. 'You're wrong, Paul. Try looking in a mirror. Ella *is* your daughter. I don't know what Gwendolyn told you but maybe she had her reasons for lying. Or maybe she didn't know. Get a DNA test if you really want the truth, but I don't think you need to worry about Louise getting custody. It won't happen.'

Paul was staring at her with an intensity that would have been frightening if Jenna didn't still feel so numb.

'And don't stop loving her,' Jenna added. 'She's never going to betray you. You're her papa. Her *father*. She loves you.'

Like she herself did. With absolute trust. So sad that, in Jenna's case, that trust was broken.

'She loves you, too,' Paul said in bewilderment. 'I don't understand any of this, Jenna.

What difference does it make? You can't leave! I'm going to marry you.'

'So you can have a mother for Ella? A nurse and companion for your mother? I heard you say you'd do anything for your family, Paul. You have already, haven't you, claiming Ella as your child when you don't really believe she is? You don't love me. Not the way you loved your first wife. You said so yourself. Chalk and cheese.'

'Of course it's not the same!' Paul ran stiff fingers through his hair, with a growling sound of frustration. 'It's—'

'It's not good enough,' Jenna interrupted. 'It could never *be* good enough. I can't marry someone who's not in love with me, Paul, no matter how I feel about you.'

'So you're *leaving*? You're *walking out* on me?'

He didn't like that. He hadn't allowed Louise to walk out on him in the library, had he? Bewilderment was giving way to anger.

'*Women!*' Paul turned back towards the lounge, walked a couple of steps but then swung back to face Jenna. 'You cannot walk out on me, Jenna,' he declared. 'I will not allow it.'

'You can't stop me.'

They stared at each other in silence.

A painful silence that seemed to grow heavier with each thump of Jenna's heart.

And then it was broken.

Not by Jenna. Or by Paul.

The sound that broke the silence was a shrill feminine scream that came from behind the lounge door.

CHAPTER ELEVEN

THE scream had come from Louise.

She was standing near the sideboard that had a bottle of bourbon lying on its side, spinning slowly as its contents dribbled onto the polished wood. She had her arms around the not insubstantial figure of Gerald and she was valiantly struggling to keep him upright.

Gerald was slumped against Louise. His face was a terrible shade of grey and he was mumbling incoherently. Maria was rushing to assist Louise as Paul threw the door open and strode into the room, with Jenna only a step behind him.

'Sit him down!' Maria ordered. 'He's fainting!'

'No…' Gerald lurched as Maria grabbed one of his arms. 'I'm… Ah-h-h! It *hurts*!'

Paul stepped in behind the trio and slipped his

arms under Gerald's. 'You can let him go,' he told Maria and Louise calmly. 'I've got him.' He began to step backwards, carefully easing Gerald to the carpeted floor.

Jenna grabbed some cushions from a couch. If Gerald wasn't actually unconscious, it would make it easier for him to breathe if he was propped up a little, rather than lying flat on the floor.

'Thanks.' Paul's acknowledgement was automatic. He expected Jenna to be there helping, didn't he? Just as *she* expected to be there. It was where she belonged. 'See what his pulse is like, would you, Jenna?'

'Oh, my God,' Louise sobbed. 'He's having another heart attack, isn't he?'

'It's possible,' Paul agreed.

'*Do* something, then!' Louise cried. 'You can't let him die!'

'Not…going…to…die…' Gerald groaned.

'Maria?' Paul looked up at his mother, who was wringing her hands in frustration at not being able to help. 'Could you find some aspirin, please? And a little water?'

Maria rushed out eagerly as Jenna knelt

opposite Paul on the other side of Gerald and felt for a pulse in his wrist.

'No radial,' she had to report.

'Blood pressure must be well down. That's hardly surprising.' Paul put his fingers on Gerald's neck. 'Carotid's faint…too fast to count.'

'VT?' Jenna's heart sank. Ventricular tachycardia was only a step away from something much worse. Something with the real potential to be fatal.

'That'd be my pick, too,' Paul agreed. He pulled a slim mobile phone from his pocket and dialled a three-digit number. 'Ambulance,' he said tersely a moment later. 'Hamilton Avenue, number 438. We've got a cardiac patient here who needs urgent transport.'

'*Oh…*' Louise was pushing against Jenna as she dropped to the floor and grasped Gerald's hand. *'Gerry!'*

Maria came back and Jenna helped him take the aspirin tablet. 'Chew it up,' she instructed. 'I'll give you a sip of water to help it go down.'

It wasn't easy and Gerald gagged at one point, which drew another distressed sound from

Louise. Then he swallowed some water and his head dropped back onto the cushions.

''S all right…babe…' he said. 'Not…gonna…die…'

'Don't even say that,' Louise begged. 'I…love you, Gerry.'

'Love you…too, babe…' Gerald's chest heaved the effort he was making to breathe. He forced his eyes open again. 'Don't forget… we're…gonna take that…world cruise…for… our honeymoon…'

'Oh-h-h!' Louise's face twisted into desolate lines and she had to hide behind her hands as she began to weep uncontrollably.

Maria tutted in shared distress and folded her arms around Louise, drawing her back to her feet. 'Don't cry,' she said. 'It will be all right. Paolo is looking after him. Paolo and Jenna. He's tough, this *amore* of yours, he's got through this before. He's still alive and where there's life, there's always hope. You'll see…it will be all right…'

Jenna bit her lip. Maybe it was because Maria was also upset and her grasp on appropriate words of encouragement might be slipping, but she was making things sound very dire. Mind you, surviving a previous heart attack was hardly the best reference either. It meant there was already damage to the heart muscle and another blow—especially a large one—could well be the final straw. Gerald was gasping for breath now and perspiration glistened on his face, but Paul stayed perfectly calm.

'Hang in there, Gerry,' he said. 'We'll get you to hospital in no time and they'll sort you out.'

'Yeah…' Gerald had to make even more of an effort to open his eyes as he slipped further towards unconsciousness. 'Thanks…mate.' He rolled his head from side to side with a groan of agony. 'Lu…?'

'I'm here, darling.' Louise broke free of Maria's hold and threw herself down to kneel beside Gerald again.

'Stay…with…me…babe…'

'Always, Gerry.' Louise sniffed inelegantly and blinked hard. 'I'm here. I'm not going anywhere. We belong together, you and me, don't we? You're going to be all right, do you hear me? Everything's going to be all right…'

The passionate and reassuring patter continued behind Jenna as she ran to the door at the sound of the approaching emergency vehicle.

The sight of her overnight bag in the hallway came as a surprise and it took a moment to realise that the current crisis had made her own misery insignificant enough to be totally forgotten. It had seemed like such a matter of life and death when she'd stood there, ready to say goodbye to Paul for ever.

How ridiculous! Jenna pulled the heavy front door open. *This* was a matter of life and death. Louise had to be feeling a lot worse than Jenna had when she'd stood here, holding that bag. Death was the ultimate separation, wasn't it? No hope of going back.

Did she have hope that somehow things would come right for herself and Paul?

Of course she did. Maria's comfort might not have been the best thing for Louise to hear but she'd been right. Where there was life there was always hope, wasn't there?

She'd hang onto that thought. Pull it out again later, perhaps, when she had the time and inclination to think about something personal. That certainly wasn't going to be any time in the immediate future.

By coincidence, it was the same paramedic team that had arrived to treat Maria's hypoglycaemic coma.

'It's not Maria, is it?' one asked as they pushed a stretcher laden with gear through the door. 'I don't remember her having a cardiac history.'

'No. This is a male patient,' Jenna told them. 'Gerry. He's a friend of...' Goodness, how could she begin to describe the complicated interconnections among this group of people she had become so involved with? 'Of...the family,' she concluded.

Not that Gerald's credentials mattered. The team went into action with commendable speed on entering the lounge.

'This is Gerald,' Paul informed them. 'He's fifty-two years old and has a prior history of MI. He collapsed ten minutes ago and was pale and diaphoretic. No radial pulse but carotid was present. Tachycardic but regular.'

'Not tachy now.' The female paramedic had already attached the electrode pads and they all stared at the screen as she took the oxygen mask from her partner and slipped it over Gerald's head.

'ST elevation,' Paul noted. 'And wide complex. Looks like complete heart block.'

'Yeah. I'll get an IV line in.'

Gerald groaned as the needle slid into a vein on his arm.

'Sorry, mate,' the paramedic said, snapping the tourniquet open. 'I'm going to give you something for that pain in just a sec.'

'He's already had aspirin,' Paul told them. 'Three hundred milligrams.'

'That's great. The sooner that's on board the better.'

Morphine was then administered. And an anti-emetic.

'Rate's down to forty-five,' one of the paramedics observed moments later. 'Gerry? Can you hear me? Open your eyes!'

Gerald's eyes remained closed. The painful stimulus of knuckles rubbing on his collar-bone failed to elicit any response.

'Draw up some atropine,' the senior paramedic ordered.

The drug was effective in bringing up the heart rate. Too effective. The rate kept increasing and then became irregular with a few odd, ectopic beats. Then it became wildly irregular. Just a frantic squiggle on the screen.

'VF,' Paul warned.

The female paramedic had her fingers on Gerald's neck. 'No pulse.'

'Right. Stand clear,' her partner ordered. 'I'm going to shock him.'

'Oh-h-h!' Louise shrieked. *'No-o-o!'*

Jenna scrambled to her feet and went to stand on one side of the distraught woman. Maria was on the other side. They both held onto Louise as she sagged at the knees—a horrified response to the jerk that Gerald's body displayed on receiving the shock.

'Look at that! We're back to sinus rhythm.' The paramedic sounded delighted.

'Let's get rolling. We need to get this guy into ED.'

Jenna left Louise with Maria to help in the whirl of activity as they gathered equipment and loaded Gerald into the ambulance.

'I'll come with you,' Paul said.

'I'm coming, too,' Louise sobbed.

The paramedics nodded appreciatively at Paul's announcement but looked a little concerned by Louise's.

'Someone going to come with her?' one asked. 'We've got room for one more.'

'You go,' Maria said firmly to Jenna. 'I will stay with Ella.'

But Jenna hesitated. What would Paul want? She had already declared her intention to leave. Would he prefer to keep his small, unusual family together in a crisis, without an outsider like her involved?

She couldn't ask, even with a questioning glance. Paul had already climbed into the back of the ambulance and was helping to untangle IV lines and electrode wires and put the oxygen tubing onto the main cylinders on full flow.

'Go,' Maria repeated. She gave Jenna a gentle shove in the direction of the door. 'You should stay with Paolo.'

Jenna responded to the shove without any

further hesitation. It was where *she* wanted to be, after all.

'Ring me,' Maria called after her, 'as soon as you know anything.'

To begin with, Jenna sat alone in the emergency department's room for waiting relatives. Paul stayed with Louise in the resuscitation area as they treated Gerald. He came back, periodically, to let Jenna know what was happening and then she would ring Maria and pass on any news.

'He's conscious again but showing some major ST elevation in his inferior leads,' Paul told Jenna.

'It looks like he *is* having another heart attack,' Jenna told Maria.

'He's getting runs of VT,' Paul reported later. 'They've started him on an IV beta-blocker.'

'He's getting drugs to control his heart rhythm,' Jenna reported to Maria.

'Big rise in cardiac enzymes,' was Paul's next information. 'We're moving him up to the lab in a few minutes.'

'They're taking him up to the cardiac catheter laboratory,' Jenna explained to Maria. 'He's going to have angioplasty, which should clear the blocked artery and stop the heart attack before it can do too much damage.'

'*Dio mio,*' Maria tutted. 'Poor Louise! You'll stay with her, won't you? While Gerry has this operation?'

'Of course. I have no idea how long it will take but I'll ring you as soon as we know how it's gone. Are you OK?'

'*Si.* I have done my finger prick and my injection and another finger prick just to check. I am fine, *cara*. You look after Louise. And Paolo. And yourself.'

They were shown another area where they could wait. A tiny room with a row of upright chairs off the corridor that led to the day-surgery wing. It was well after normal working hours now and this area of the hospital felt deserted. So quiet they could hear the ticking of the clock on the wall of the small space. One of the chairs had some well-out-of-date magazines covering its seat but nobody took any notice.

They sat there, the three of them, in a rather strained silence. Jenna sat in the middle. Her offer to go searching for coffee or food had been declined. Another minute ticked by. And another. She took a glance to her right.

Louise looked dreadful. She had a box of tissues on her lap that had probably come from the emergency department. It was a square island in a sea of crumpled, used tissues now. Her normally immaculate hair was a mess and mascara streaks showed up vividly on her pale cheeks. No hint of lipstick remained on her lips and even the once matching nail polish was vanishing as she chewed one nail after another.

Jenna thought about offering to hold Louise's hand to comfort her. Then she thought about trying to hold Paul's hand...to comfort herself. She stole a glance to her left but Paul was sitting with his head resting on the wall behind them, his eyes closed.

Jenna followed his example with a sigh.

They needed to talk but it wasn't a conversation they could have here. Paul would hardly thank her for broaching such a private subject in front of

Louise, would he? And it was hardly the time to cause Louise any further upset by reopening the topic she had overheard in the library.

It was a time of waiting. For all of them.

So they sat in this uncomfortable silence. Together and yet completely separate.

The wait seemed interminable.

Paul kept his eyes shut and gritted his teeth. He had to be there because, whether he liked it or not, Louise was a part of his family and was therefore entitled to his assistance and protection.

The frustration was unbearable. He desperately needed to talk to Jenna and convince her that she had taken an incorrect interpretation from what she had heard, but he couldn't desert Louise yet. Not until Gerald came out of the lab, hopefully with a good result.

And he certainly couldn't say anything that might invite Louise to threaten Jenna in any way. Not that she looked like much of a threat at this moment, but Paul knew Jenna would do a great deal to protect both Maria and Ella. If she thought that agreeing to marry him would cause grief to people she cared about so much, it could be enough to tip what was now a precarious balance.

Louise didn't know that their conversation in the library had been overheard and so she couldn't know how close she was to getting what she wanted—the cancellation of any marriage plans between himself and Jenna.

Paul couldn't get rid of the mental image of that bag in the hallway of his house. The symbol of Jenna's intention to walk out of his life. Maybe the balance had already tipped too far. Maybe he had already lost Jenna.

He couldn't understand it.

What better time to replay in his head that unpleasant conversation in the library? Again and again. Trying to find the interpretation Jenna had taken from his words.

Yes, he'd said that Maria and Ella both adored Jenna. It was true. And she loved them, didn't she? So how could that be a problem?

Yes, he'd said she had become a part of the family and he'd said that his family mattered to him above all else.

Also true. How could he say with any more conviction just how important Jenna was to him?

Family was *everything*.

He'd never felt like that about Gwendolyn. She'd been a very beautiful woman and he'd been overwhelmingly attracted to her, but she'd never *belonged* with him.

Not the way Jenna did.

For the first time Paul could understand what had gone wrong before and why he felt the way he did about Jenna. It went so much deeper than merely being 'in love'. It was about trust. Genuine commitment. A need to protect but, more than that, the trust that you could be protected yourself.

You could be vulnerable but safe at the same time.

Would Jenna understand that feeling? Would it help if he told her?

He *had* to tell her.

Paul opened his eyes and turned his head. Perhaps he could communicate something of what he was thinking through eye contact. A willingness to explain, perhaps. Appreciation that she was still here beside him, at least.

But Jenna's eyes were closed and her head drifting slowly sideways. Paul shifted his body weight so that her shoulder touched his arm. So that there was something solid for her head to rest against while she dozed.

Jenna slowly became aware of the voices.

She knew it was Louise and that she was talking to Paul, but the conversation had a dream-like quality to it. This was no argument. Louise sounded husky. Totally sincere. Almost broken.

She shouldn't be listening but, once again, Jenna appeared to be inadvertently part of a private conversation.

'You don't have to say it, Paul. I know how little you think of me.'

'You've never made it easy, Louise. I *did* try, you know, at first…'

'I had to take Gwen's side. She was my daughter.'

'I know.'

'I hate to say it but…she didn't deserve you…'

'Scusi?'

Jenna felt the sudden tension in Paul's body.

She pressed her cheek against his shoulder, as though stirring in her sleep, and then she felt a different touch as he tilted his head to rest against hers. As though he was curling around her. To protect *her*, even when it seemed that Louise might be about to launch a new verbal offensive against *him*.

Except she wasn't.

'You're a good man, Paul.' Louise sniffed and then blew her nose. 'Thank you for helping with Gerry and for…for being here with me like this.'

'You're very welcome.'

'I really do love him, you know.' Louise sounded like she was struggling not to cry again. 'I know what you think of me and it's true that I've used men in the past, but this is *so* different.'

'Is it?'

'I know he's not perfect but neither am I—as you pointed out yourself today—but you know what? Gerry *loves* me. He really loves me and it makes me feel like I'm *worth* loving. It's taken more than forty years but for the first time in my life I've discovered what love really is, can you believe that?'

'Oh, yes,' Paul murmured. 'I can believe it.'

'He can't die.' Louise sniffed again and Jenna heard the sound of another tissue being ripped from the box. 'I want to spend the rest of my life with him. I want it so much.'

Louise unsuccessfully tried to stifle a sob and Jenna felt her heart squeeze. She knew exactly how Louise was feeling. It was how she felt about Paul, wasn't it?

'I'm sorry,' Louise croaked. 'I shouldn't be telling you all this. I mean, why should you even care?'

'I care,' Paul said quietly. 'And I do understand, Louise.'

'You do?'

'Of course I do. It's precisely the way I feel about Jenna.'

Jenna's eyes flew open quite involuntarily. And her hand moved. Or had Paul's moved first? Their fingers touched and then intertwined, their hands joining like two bubbles of mercury finding each other. A completely fluid action that would have been impossible to resist.

'Well, why didn't you say so?' Louise sounded puzzled.

'I did.'

'No, you didn't. You said you hadn't fallen for her…not like you did for Gwen.'

'I did say that,' Paul agreed. 'And it's true. I fell for Gwen, Louise. So hard I hit my head and couldn't think straight. It was accidental and… sadly it turned out to be superficial. For both of us.'

He shifted his head to look down at Jenna and seemed unsurprised to find her staring back at him. Of course, he must have known she was awake as soon as their hands touched.

'This time,' Paul said softly, holding her gaze, 'I knew exactly what I was doing. I knew the potholes that kind of road could have and I thought long and hard before I stepped onto it. This was no accident.'

He looked up, presumably straight at Louise. 'I'm not going to forget Gwen,' he said sombrely. 'How could I when she was responsible for bringing Ella into the world? Even if I'm not her genetic father, it makes no difference because I have come to love her…very much.'

'She could have been wrong,' Louise said. 'She was never very good with her dates about things.'

'*Non importa.* She is family now. And you, Louise, you will always have a place in my family as well. As Ella's other *nonna*. But Jenna's place is the most important because she holds the heart of the family. She holds *my* heart and we belong together. Just the way you and Gerry belong together.' His gaze locked with Jenna's again.

'*Ti amo, dolcissima. Amore mio.* I love you. Now and for ever.'

Jenna's eyes blurred with tears. Joyous tears. 'I love you, too,' she whispered.

'You forgive me, then? For saying whatever it was I said that upset you so much?'

'I didn't understand properly, that's all.'

'Maybe I didn't either.' Paul smiled. That delicious slow smile that started with a crinkle of his eyes and finished with a warmth that chased away any dark patches in Jenna's soul. 'I'm still learning. You taught me a lesson, Jenna. I *never* want to see a bag in my hallway again.'

Jenna smiled back. 'You won't,' she promised.

'*Oh!*' Louise sucked in a nervous breath. 'Someone's coming!'

'They'll be just down here!' The cheerful voice of a nurse could be heard coming from the dimly lit corridor. 'There's a little waiting room. See?'

'*Grazie, grazie!*' A small, plump figure appeared through the doorway.

'Maria!' Jenna scrambled to her feet and Paul stood up beside her, still holding her hand. 'Is Ella all right? Are *you* all right?'

'We are fine. You didn't call, *cara*, and I was worried so I called a taxi and, *poof*! Here we are! A family needs to be together at a time like this, does it not, Paolo?'

'Indeed it does,' Paul agreed solemnly.

'Take your daughter,' Maria instructed. 'She is getting heavy.'

Paul took the bundle that was Ella wrapped in a blanket from Maria's arms and Jenna took the basket the nurse had been carrying.

'I brought food,' Maria said unnecessarily. A very appetising smell was coming from the basket. 'Lasagne. And bread. Enough for us all.'

Louise was on her feet now as well. She caught the arm of the nurse. 'Could you possibly go in there?' She waved through the doorway to the double doors excluding them from the day surgery area. 'Could you find out what's happening with Gerry? How much longer it might be before we hear anything?'

'Sure.' The nurse hurried off.

Jenna rearranged the blanket so it didn't cover Ella's face. Letto's legs were poking out at an awkward angle but when she tried to straighten the toy, Ella's face scrunched ominously and she made a soft growling sound.

'So grumpy!' Maria smiled fondly. 'You were just the same, Paolo, when *you* were a *bambino*.' She sat down on one of the chairs and fanned her face with her hand. 'So hot, these hospitals,' she complained. 'Why is that?'

But nobody answered because they had heard the swish of the double doors opening again. The nurse they had sent as a messenger reappeared—with company.

'Good news,' the cardiologist told them all. 'Perfect procedure. He's got a bit of extra plumbing in there now but all signs of the infarct have resolved.'

'What does that mean?' Louise had a hand to her throat. 'Is he…going to be all right?'

'Probably in better nick now than he's been for years,' the cardiologist said. 'Are you his partner?' His mouth twitched only a little. 'Lulu?'

Louise nodded, clearly unable to say anything.

'He's asking for you.' The cardiologist grinned. 'In fact, he's *been* asking for you at about sixty-second intervals ever since he went in.' The doctor paused and sniffed appreciatively. 'Something smells awfully good in here.'

'It's my lasagne,' Maria said proudly. 'You want some?'

'No!' Louise clutched at his arm. '*Please*! Take me to see Gerry.'

Maria watched as Louise disappeared through the door. Then she looked up to where Paul and Jenna were standing so close together, with the sleeping baby between them, staring into each other's eyes. Their love was as obvious as the aroma of the hot food wafting from her basket.

Maria nodded with enormous satisfaction. All was well in her world.

Very well. There had been no need to fret so much about that bag in the hallway.

'Come,' she ordered her family. 'Eat!'

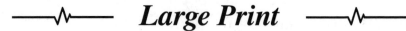

MEDICAL™

Large Print

Titles for the next six months…

October

THE DOCTOR'S ROYAL LOVE-CHILD   Kate Hardy
HIS ISLAND BRIDE   Marion Lennox
A CONSULTANT BEYOND COMPARE   Joanna Neil
THE SURGEON BOSS'S BRIDE   Melanie Milburne
A WIFE WORTH WAITING FOR   Maggie Kingsley
DESERT PRINCE, EXPECTANT MOTHER Olivia Gates

November

NURSE BRIDE, BAYSIDE WEDDING   Gill Sanderson
BILLIONAIRE DOCTOR, ORDINARY   Carol Marinelli
NURSE
THE SHEIKH SURGEON'S BABY   Meredith Webber
THE OUTBACK DOCTOR'S SURPRISE BRIDE Amy Andrews
A WEDDING AT LIMESTONE COAST   Lucy Clark
THE DOCTOR'S MEANT-TO-BE MARRIAGE   Janice Lynn

December

SINGLE DAD SEEKS A WIFE   Melanie Milburne
HER FOUR-YEAR BABY SECRET   Alison Roberts
COUNTRY DOCTOR, SPRING BRIDE   Abigail Gordon
MARRYING THE RUNAWAY BRIDE   Jennifer Taylor
THE MIDWIFE'S BABY   Fiona McArthur
THE FATHERHOOD MIRACLE   Margaret Barker

MILLS & BOON®
Pure reading pleasure™

0908 LP 2P P1 Medical

MEDICAL™

⎯∿⎯ *Large Print* ⎯∿⎯

January

VIRGIN MIDWIFE, PLAYBOY DOCTOR	Margaret McDonagh
THE REBEL DOCTOR'S BRIDE	Sarah Morgan
THE SURGEON'S SECRET BABY WISH	Laura Iding
PROPOSING TO THE CHILDREN'S DOCTOR	Joanna Neil
EMERGENCY: WIFE NEEDED	Emily Forbes
ITALIAN DOCTOR, FULL-TIME FATHER	Dianne Drake

February

THEIR MIRACLE BABY	Caroline Anderson
THE CHILDREN'S DOCTOR AND THE SINGLE MUM	Lilian Darcy
THE SPANISH DOCTOR'S LOVE-CHILD	Kate Hardy
PREGNANT NURSE, NEW-FOUND FAMILY	Lynne Marshall
HER VERY SPECIAL BOSS	Anne Fraser
THE GP'S MARRIAGE WISH	Judy Campbell

March

SHEIKH SURGEON CLAIMS HIS BRIDE	Josie Metcalfe
A PROPOSAL WORTH WAITING FOR	Lilian Darcy
A DOCTOR, A NURSE: A LITTLE MIRACLE	Carol Marinelli
TOP-NOTCH SURGEON, PREGNANT NURSE	Amy Andrews
A MOTHER FOR HIS SON	Gill Sanderson
THE PLAYBOY DOCTOR'S MARRIAGE PROPOSAL	Fiona Lowe

™ MILLS & BOON®
Pure reading pleasure™

0908 LP 2P P2 Medical